# Squirrel

*Soulless Kings MC*

## Andi Rhodes

Blue Journey Publishing

Copyright © 2022 by Andi Rhodes

All rights reserved.

No part of this book may be reproduced in any form or by any electronic or mechanical means, including information storage and retrieval systems, without written permission from the author, except for the use of brief quotations in a book review.

Cover Artwork - © Amanda Walker PA & Design Services

# Also by Andi Rhodes

**Broken Rebel Brotherhood**

Broken Souls

Broken Innocence

Broken Boundaries

Broken Rebel Brotherhood: Complete Series Box set

**Broken Rebel Brotherhood: Next Generation**

Broken Hearts

Broken Wings

Broken Mind

**Bastards and Badges**

Stark Revenge

Slade's Fall

Jett's Guard

**Soulless Kings MC**

Fender

Joker

Piston

Greaser

Riker

Trainwreck

Squirrel

Gibson

**Satan's Legacy MC**

Snow's Angel

Toga's Demons

Magic's Torment

# Prologue

*If they can't drink with me, they can't fuck with me. That's always been my motto. I've never broken that rule of mine. Never.*

**Squirrel**

"Are you seeing this?"

I pause mid-clap to look at Gibson. The giant grin he's sporting is comical, and yet, I wish I could mimic it. Don't get me wrong, I'm happy for our brother, Trainwreck, and his now fiancée, Sylvia. I really am. But I'm certainly not envious.

Lately, it seems one brother after another is tying the knot, and all I can do is pray I don't get bit by that bug. I'm perfectly content to jump from one chick to the next. Keeps things interesting.

Lost in my own thoughts—memories, really—about the Bangin' Betty I hooked up with two nights ago, I'm startled when the side door to the clubhouse flies open with a bang.

"Get down on the ground. Now!"

It's as if someone took a bucket of ice and tossed it over the party: everyone freezes.

The intruders, all carrying weapons, move their way to surround the room. Only a few weave in and out of all the bodies now dropping to the floor. Then there are those of us who refuse to submit.

I catch a glimpse of the white lettering on both the front and back of the black jackets they're wearing, and my blood boils. FBI and SWAT.

*What the fuck?*

"We're looking for Travis 'Squirrel' Kramer. Where is he?" the one who seems to be leading the pack shouts.

*What the double fuck?*

Before I have a chance to say or do anything, Fender steps forward. "What is this about?"

"Sir, get down on the ground."

"With all due respect, I know my rights. I'm unarmed, my hands are in the air where you can see them, and I'm only asking a question. What do you want with Squirrel?"

"We'll discuss that with him, sir."

"Fender, it's okay," I say, and my voice seems to boom through the room. I address the SWAT team next, hands raised so there's no confusion about my intent. "I'm Travis. Also unarmed."

"Get on your knees," the agent commands. "Now."

As I drop to my knees, I put my hands on the back of my head. I've been down this road before, so I know the drill.

Another SWAT team member—Perez, according to his badge—rushes forward and around me to yank my hands from my head to behind my back.

"Travis 'Squirrel' Kramer, you're under arrest for the

murder of Maria Sampson. You have the right to remain silent..."

I know my rights, so I tune him out. Instead, I focus on the name Maria Sampson. I don't know anyone by that name, alias or otherwise. Shit, I know when I take the life of someone, and I sure as hell haven't taken hers.

*Who is she?*

"Squirrel, you say nothing until Alan gets there, you hear me? He won't be too far behind you." Fender calls out to me as I'm hauled out of the clubhouse. I hope he's right. We pay our attorney good money to be at our beck and call. "Not a word."

A man dressed in a black suit passes me just outside the doorway, but I'm being held so tightly, I'm unable to turn around and see who he walks to or hear what he says.

When we reach one of the numerous vehicles, Perez slams me against the side and pushes my head into the metal.

Instead of giving into the pain, I use it to fuel me. I twist my head as much as I can so I can see the man out of the corner of my eye.

"Pretty sure that's police brutality." I smirk at the way his eyes light up with fire at my words. "Just sayin'."

"Keep it up, Kramer." He yanks on my arms as if to prove that he's got the upper hand. "I know the guys where you're going will love that smart mouth."

I roll my eyes, used to the verbal flexing. Being the computer geek of the Soulless Kings MC means I've been through this spiel with almost every alphabet agency there is, as well as local and county police. I hack shit... a lot.

"Perez, get him in the car." Another agent slides into the driver's seat. "We've got a long drive ahead of us."

Perez does as he's told while mumbling under his breath

about how this is his arrest, and he should be running the show.

*Good to know. Prick has an ego and feels like his toes are being crushed by undeserving feet.*

"And here I thought you were in charge," I say, feeding into his frustration. "Looks can be deceiving, I guess." I wink at him after he gets me situated in the back seat. "Good info to keep in mind."

"Are you threa—"

"Perez!" the other agent barks. "Get in the goddamn car."

Perez shoots me one last glare before slamming the door and stomping around the vehicle. I don't bother trying to hide my chuckle.

"He's not wrong," the agent in the driver's seat says, meeting my eyes in the rearview mirror. "I suggest you take the day and a half ahead of us to think about how you want to play this. Murder is serious business, but factor in the age of the victim..." He shrugs. "It complicates things for you."

Instantly, I sober. I search my mind for how I know Maria Simpson, where I may have come in contact with her. But the whole age thing is throwing me for a loop. I may be a player, but I don't mess with anyone under the age of twenty-one.

If they can't drink with me, they can't fuck with me. That's always been my motto. I've never broken that rule of mine. *Never.*

After Perez joins us in the vehicle, no time is wasted before we're driving out of the compound. The car is eerily quiet, which doesn't help the spiraling trip my brain is taking. I don't know how long we're cruising past traffic, but something the agent said registers and raises an important question.

I lean forward as much as I can. "Hey, you said something about taking a day and a half to think about things. Where the hell are you taking me?"

Perez twists slightly to face me. His eyes narrow as he stares at me for a moment, almost as if he doesn't believe for a second that I don't know.

*Of course he believes that. They all do, or I wouldn't have been cuffed and stuffed into this fucking car.*

"Michigan," Perez finally says. "We're taking you to Michigan."

# Chapter One

*They matter. Unfortunately, only until they don't if I lose the case.*

**Lexi**

"Lexi!"

I pull my head out of the file it's buried in and shove my glasses up my nose as I peer at Joseph Hinton, the Chief Public Defender and an ass. For the last ten months, he's been my boss and the reason I now keep my apartment stocked with wine.

"Sorry, Mr. Hinton." I force a smile to ease his annoyance at my lack of attention. "What can I do for you?"

"My office, now."

He storms across the room to his giant corner office. He remains next to the door, tapping his toes, and waits for me while I grab a pen and pad of paper off my desk and rush to join him.

"Have a seat, Miss Cantor." He gestures to one of the two chairs typically reserved for clients and moves to sit in his creamy white leather chair behind his desk.

I sit, crossing one leg over the other, and start tugging my skirt down. Normally, I'd wear dress pants and a blouse, but I had court this morning. I always try to look a little nicer when I'm going into a courtroom.

"Stop fidgeting," he commands.

"Yes, sir," I say as I still.

*Prick.*

Mr. Hinton digs through some files on his desk until he finds what he's looking for. "I've got a new case for you." He opens the file and scans through the contents. "Pretty straight forward. Definitely not a winnable case, but you should be able to get a plea deal for him. I just need you to talk him into whatever the prosecutor offers him."

He closes the folder and hands it to me across his desk. I try not to take offense to him assuming I can't win the case, but it's hard. I graduated at the top of my class at Harvard Law School, and I've won my fair share of cases. Sure, I lose some too, but those are the ones who are truly guilty and deserve what's coming to them.

And then I open the file.

*First degree murder? Of a fourteen-year-old girl? What the hell is he thinking?*

"Sir, not that I don't want the case, but wouldn't you prefer someone with a bit more experience? Someone who's actually handled a murder case before?"

Mr. Hinton sits forward in his chair, leaning his forearms on the edge of his desk. He steeples his fingers and stares at me for a beat too long before relaxing, trying to create a more agreeable environment, no doubt.

"Here's the thing, Lexi. I need someone who's going to go in there and do what they're told. This case needs to be closed quickly, and a plea deal is the way to do that. I

*Squirrel*

figured you're my best bet to get that done. Is that going to be a problem?"

There's something in his tone, something that feels like I need to be reading between the lines. Very blurry lines at that. Mr. Hinton is a stickler for closing cases, but typically he wants to place them in the win column, not the 'get it closed no matter what the cost' column.

"No, sir." I shake my head. "No problem."

"Good." He stands from his chair, indicating that this meeting is over, and I follow suit. "You meet with your client tomorrow, after they've had a chance to process him into the facility. I suggest you familiarize yourself with the case so you know the best way to carry this to the end."

"Yes, sir." I turn to walk out of the office but stop to look over my shoulder once I reach the door. "The meeting is already set, sir?"

He nods.

"For what time?"

"Eight. His arraignment is at noon. That should give you plenty of time to prep."

*It gives me no time.*

I keep that thought to myself for two reasons: he knows it's not 'plenty of time', and no matter how much time, it's never enough. An attorney can always use more time. Especially one who's stretched thin to begin with.

"Yes, sir, plenty of time."

With that, I exit his office and walk to my desk. I nod politely to my colleagues as I pass them, but no words are exchanged. They don't see me as their equal, but instead as a newbie, fresh out of college, with no idea what she's doing. No matter. They'll see eventually. I'll make them see.

I spend the last three hours of my day diving into the case, familiarizing myself with Travis Kramer, my client.

The biggest take away I have is that this case is anything but straightforward.

At precisely five o'clock, everyone starts packing up to go home. They all have that mindset where doing only the minimal amount of work is enough. When they're done for the day, they're done. They all stay late when they have to, but they also do everything they can to not have to. And when they do, there's nothing but conversations complaining about the long hours.

I begin to pack up my stuff, knowing I have hours left ahead of me if I want to be ready for my eight o'clock appointment at the jail in the morning. When I'm sure I have everything I need, I leave the building to find my car in the parking garage across the street.

It isn't hard to spot the old, faded yellow mustang. I've had that thing since I was sixteen. Somehow, I'd managed to save enough money to buy it from a neighbor back in the Bronx. I managed to keep it running through high school, undergrad, and law school. And I need to keep it going for a little bit longer before I can get something newer.

I slide into the driver's side and toss my bag onto the passenger's seat. After starting the engine, I lean back and take a few minutes to simply breathe before I face traffic and a long night of work at home.

Memories flood my mind. The day I graduated high school and the look of pride my parents wore. They both had that same look with each of my graduations, but especially when I finished law school. I rode that high for a few months, until it became clear that my education alone wasn't going to get me a job.

My parents begged me to look for a position as a prosecutor, but that's not where my heart was. It still isn't. Ever since I can remember, I wanted to be a public defender. So

## Squirrel

when I got my first offer in Michigan, I jumped at the chance. And I love it, despite my asshole boss.

I shake my head free of my thoughts. It doesn't do me a damn bit of good to dwell on the way my parents' pride disappeared when I took the job, how the light in their eyes dimmed when I loaded up my beat-up car to move to a different state.

Looking back, I recognize now why they were, and still are, so upset. They saw me as a meal ticket, as a way to get out of the Bronx and have a better life, a more comfortable life. I see it so clearly now, and it's only reinforced with every awkward phone call.

Once again, I push my thoughts aside. I focus on backing out of the parking space and driving home. It doesn't take long as I only live about ten miles from the office building. Sure, traffic adds a little time, but it's not such a huge city that I'm stuck in the car for hours.

Forty minutes later, I pull into the parking lot of my complex and navigate my way to my building. The complex isn't exactly what someone might picture for someone with a law degree, but it's affordable and allows pets. I hadn't necessarily planned on getting one, but I'm glad I did. I don't know what I'd do without my boxer, Bug. He's a big lug, but with him, I don't feel so lonely.

I hear Bug's paws padding on the tile floor on the other side of the door, and when I swing it open, he jumps up to greet me.

"Hey, Bug," I manage to spit out between his sloppy kisses. "Did ya miss me? Huh?"

I give his ears a good scratch before gently pushing him down so I can close the door and settle in. Bug waits by the door, like he always does, while I put my bags down and then change into a pair of leggings and hoodie so I can take him for a walk. This has been our routine from the first day I brought him home from the rescue, and if we stray from it at all, he lets me know.

When I return to his side, he's sitting with the end of his leash, which hangs on the wall by the door, in his mouth. I reach for it, and he drops it into my hand.

"Good boy," I croon as I attach it to his wide collar. "Such a good boy."

I lead him outside, and we walk for an hour. Occasionally his attention is pulled in random directions as he spots squirrels or birds or anything he sees move. He doesn't chase anything, but he wants to.

After returning home and making sure he has food and water, I make myself a peanut butter and jelly sandwich and fill a glass with the cheap boxed wine in the refrigerator. I sling my bag over my shoulder and carry everything to the living room, where I plop down on the couch.

It doesn't take me more than a few minutes to finish my sandwich and almost drain my glass. But I don't bother getting more... yet. Right now, I need to work.

As I log into my laptop, Bug jumps up on the couch and does a few circles before flopping down and laying his head against my thigh. I run a hand over his fur while I wait for my computer to load.

Two minutes later, I'm scrolling through social media, trying to find all I can on Travis Kramer. In the file it listed an association with a motorcycle called Soulless Kings MC. I've been unable to find much on them, other than what law enforcement databases provided me. Oh, and a few articles written by a Holland Tibideaux-Best. Although I take those with a grain of salt because a quick search revealed she's married to Sam 'Piston' Best, the club's VP.

## Squirrel

It's all relevant, but at the same time, not exactly what I'm looking for.

In order to properly defend a client, I need to know who they are as a person. Most attorneys would probably tell me it's a waste of time, but I disagree. When defending a person against a crime, especially murder, everything from the second they were born to the day of court matters. They matter. Unfortunately, only until they don't if I lose the case.

*Plea deal. That's what you're supposed to be focused on.*

I hear the instructions my boss gave me. They play on a loop like a rollercoaster ride, only this is a ride I hope breaks down. I don't want to do what he wants. Not this time. If for no other reason than my clients deserve my best and nothing less. They deserve an attorney who's open to the possibility that they're innocent. And if they *are* innocent, a plea deal is less than my best.

With that in mind, I dig deeper, as deep as I can go. I find as much as I can because I know I need to walk into that jail tomorrow with a warrior attitude.

If I'm going to defend a member of an MC and go against my boss's orders, I'm gonna need it.

# Chapter Two

*Miss Cantor is a feisty one. And I like it.*

**Squirrel**

I wrap my hands around the bars of my temporary cell and listen for my name to be called. When breakfast —if runny eggs and a blackened, dry as hell English muffin can be called that—was delivered, the guard let me know I'd be pulled to meet with a public defender this morning. Of course, he said it with a sneer, as if tickled by the fact that I can't afford any better.

*Newsflash, motherfucker, I can. But for some reason, I wasn't given a choice.*

Rolling my neck, I catch sight of the navy-blue jumpsuit they gave me at intake. I hate the thing. I'm covered completely, but I couldn't possibly feel more naked. When they took my cut, I fought so hard the guard ended up having to tase me. Needless to say, that didn't help my attitude any. But it did what it was intended to do, and I stopped fighting. They'll get what's coming to them. Maybe not by my hands, but I hear karma is a bitch.

"Kramer!"

I perk up at the sound of my name, and when the cell door starts to slide open, I drop my arms and wait for the guard to come handcuff me. The concrete and metal space is filled with the yells of other inmates, some directed at me but most directed at the guards. I try to ignore it, but it's impossible with the way it echoes off the walls, bouncing all around me.

As I'm led out of the pod and down a long hall, the sounds become distant, and I finally feel like I can formulate a complete thought. Unfortunately, the thoughts are so jumbled because there are so many of them.

Who is Maria Sampson?

Why am I meeting with a public defender and not the club attorney?

When the hell was I in Michigan?

Question after question swirls through my mind like a tornado ripping apart a community without discrimination. But the last one to pop up is the one I speak aloud.

"Why haven't I gotten my one phone call?"

The guard stops walking and turns to stare at me.

"You're in here for murder and that's what you're worried about?"

"I'm in here for a murder I didn't fucking commit, and I'm concerned about my basic civil rights," I grit out. "What happened to innocent until proven guilty?"

The guard yanks me forward and we start walking again before he says, "Trash like you happened."

*What the fuck?*

Rather than continue to engage in conversation, I keep my mouth shut for the rest of the walk. I'm led through several metal detectors before being shoved into a small room and shackled to the table.

Other than the table and two chairs, the room is empty. No mirrored wall, which I realize is to ensure attorney-client privilege. I sit there for I don't know how long, alone and left to stew in my own head.

After what seems like an eternity, the door slowly opens and in walks...

*You've gotta be fucking kidding me.*

"Sorry I'm late."

The woman struggles to hang onto the coffee in her hand, a thick file, and her bag. When she settles everything onto the table and finally lifts her head to look at me, my breath catches.

*She's gorgeous, in an uptight, girl next door sorta way. And... young.*

"Is this a joke or somethin'?" The words are out of my mouth before they even register in my brain.

She pushes her black-rimmed glasses up her nose and pulls out the chair across from me. "Excuse me?"

The corners of my mouth tug up at her indignant tone, but I quickly mask it. I do allow my eyes to roam over her from her loosely styled coffee-brown hair to the tidy suit she's wearing. She looks like she's trying to hide her true self from the world, and if I were anywhere but here, I'd be teasing her out of hiding.

But *because* of where I am, I keep my guard up and don't let myself appear to be doing anything but gawking at her like a pervert.

"You can't be older than..." I flap a hand at her as best I can with the cuffs. "Well, not old enough to be a lawyer. Certainly not one who can defend me against the fucking charges I'm up against."

"I beg your—"

"You sure are nice to look at though." I leer at her, although I can't be sure it's not coming across as a teasing grin. She's got my brain more muddled than I'd like. "At least they got that right."

Her face hardens. She glares at me as she rests her hands on the table and leans toward me.

"I'm only going to say this once, Mr. Kramer." She tilts her head. "You can sit here and pretend to be a hard ass, but it won't get you anywhere. I have a job to do, and you don't scare me."

The slight shake in her arms gives the lie away. I scare the shit out of her, as I should. But that doesn't stop the fraction of respect she's gained by trying to stand up to me. I lean toward her, and, to her credit, she doesn't flinch.

"Do you have any idea who I am?"

I speak through gritted teeth, with a slight growl, and when her pupils dilate, my cock swells beneath the jumpsuit.

"As a matter of fact..." Standing up straight, she lifts a file into her hands and opens it. "You're thirty-two-year-old Travis Kramer, although you go by Squirrel, a name given to you by the Soulless Kings MC. You reside in Oregon on your club's compound. You've got a history of arrests for multiple crimes, but the most common is hacking databases and servers that no civilian should have access to. Which is why you handle the more technical stuff for the club. You also have a juvenile record, and while it's sealed, *I too* have my ways to get what I want. You were arrested at fifteen and charged with the death of another teenager. It was a case of 'wrong place, wrong time'. Charges were dismissed." She glances up from the documents and smirks at me. "Shall I go on?"

Shocked by the amount of information she has, I stay silent.

"Okay then." She looks back down and flips to a second page. "According to the police report, you're six foot one, two hundred and twenty-eight pounds, have nineteen tattoos, and a scar on your upper left thigh from what was reported as a domestic violence incident. You were not the aggressor, and in fact, weren't the aggressor in all three incidents reported to police with the same woman."

She closes the file and tosses it down onto the table. When she crosses her arms over her chest, I force my eyes to stay on her face and not the cleavage she's pushing up. I know that the information she has is a problem. She knows more about me than some of my brothers. But again, I find myself respecting her for it and not wanting to tear her apart... well, not in an angry sort of way.

I could definitely do a number on her, but one that would end with her screaming my name as she comes, not as she reads me the riot act for being an asshole.

"Clearly, you've done your homework," I admit. "And yet, none of that proves to me that you're qualified to defend me against murder charges."

The firecracker in a confident, buttoned-down facade rolls her eyes at me. "And what can I do to prove that I'm qualified?"

I think about it for a minute, although the answer is simple: win the damn case. But that's not what I say. Instead, for reasons unknown, I decide to mess with her.

"I don't know." I shrug. "Give me your name for starters. Maybe follow that with your actual qualifications. "Oh, and I don't know, how about fill me in on what you know about the fucking case. Yeah, that'd be a start. Then when you're done with that, tell me the color of your panties and bra size." I grin when her cheeks pinken, and I snap my fingers. "No wait, don't tell me that last one." I dip my head to her chest for a beat too long before looking back at her face. "D cup?"

I lean back in my chair and wait for her to gain some composure. I threw her for a loop, if the color of her cheeks and the way she's fidgeting with her hands is any indication. Good. If she's going to help me walk out of here a free man, she needs to be on her toes. If I can rattle her, a prosecutor or uncooperative witness can too. And that would only end in bad things for me.

She squares her shoulders and pins me with her stare. "My name is Lexi Cantor. I received my law degree from Harvard, graduated top of my class. I've been with the public defender's office for ten months and have a very good track record. That speaks to my qualifications." She finally sits down in the chair. "My panties are green, and my bra size is a thirty-two D. And here's a little free piece of info… green is also my favorite color, and I love chocolate chip cookies." She pauses to push her glasses up her nose. "As for what I know about the case? Everything. I know everything."

The tension drains from my body. Miss Cantor is a feisty one. And I like it.

"Good."

I scoot forward in my chair.

"Care to fill me in, because I don't know shit?"

# Chapter Three

*I'm left to wonder just how much the chips are stacked against me, against Squirrel.*

**Lexi**

My stomach is in knots as I sit at the defense table. The prosecutor is Gregory Firth, who is known for his ruthlessness in the courtroom, not to mention the speculation that he doesn't fight fair and some of his cases are rigged. Then there's Judge Ruth Belmont. She specializes in crimes against children and never hesitates to deliver the harshest sentences she can to those who perpetrate them.

Also in the courtroom are several men wearing leather vests. Each sports a scowl directed at the prosecutor. I assume they're here for Squirrel, if the patches on their vests mean anything, but one can never be sure of these things. Regardless, their presence has caused the air in the room to feel thin and the space much smaller.

As if that isn't enough pressure, I'm stuck sitting next to a man who is the reason I had to go home before court and change my panties just so I wasn't wearing green ones. The man who my first thought when meeting him was 'holy shit, his pictures don't do him justice'.

*What possessed me to tell him the color of my underwear and my bra size?*

Travis Kramer is also the man who I'm supposed to convince to take a plea deal. Problem is, I think he's innocent, which forces me to figure out whether or not to follow orders or my gut.

"Miss Cantor?"

I lift my head and look at Judge Belmont. "Your Honor?"

"How does your client plead?"

I turn to face Mr. Kramer—Squirrel, as he insisted I call him at our earlier meeting—and raise a brow. Before we concluded our conversation at the jail, I filled him in on the evidence the prosecution has against him, which is very little. We discussed his options in detail. Unfortunately, I couldn't say whether or not the prosecution is willing to deal, but I laid out that option anyway.

Squirrel gives a curt nod. I'm either about to make a huge mistake and a killer will be set free, or my gut is right and I'm going to help set free an innocent man. Not to mention the implications for my career, no matter how this goes.

I return my attention to the judge and stand. "Not guilty, Your Honor."

Judge Belmont nods and shifts her head to look at Squirrel. "Mr. Kramer, is this correct?"

Squirrel stands, his hands still cuffed in front of him. "Yes, Your Honor."

"Okay. Let the record reflect that Mr. Kramer is pleading not guilty. He will be remanded into custody, without bail, until his trial date." She flips through the pages of what I know is her schedule. Most of the judges use the computer system; however, Judge Belmont is old-school and prefers to schedule all her own trials and have it later entered into the online calendar. "How's four weeks from today work for everyone?"

*Four weeks?!*

Gregory Firth stands. "That is acceptable to the prosecution, Your Honor."

Caught off guard with the short time frame, I pretend to scour through my own schedule in order to buy myself time to respond.

"Miss Cantor, I don't have all day," the judge admonishes with annoyance.

"Of course not, Your Honor." I stand up straight and fold my hands in front of me. "The defense requests more time, Your Honor. Four weeks is not sufficient time to prepare for a case of this magnitude."

"How much more time?" she grates out. "And please keep in mind that, without bail, there's only a ninety-day window to begin proceedings."

I glance at Squirrel, who now looks upset with me, and swallow past the lump in my throat.

"Uh, Your Honor, ninety days should be sufficient," I finally respond. I have no idea if that's enough time or not, but she's right, it's the only option.

Judge Belmont looks at her schedule again before returning her gaze to me. "I can give you four weeks."

The date is set, and court is adjourned. I remain standing there, dumbfounded. How in the hell am I supposed to defend this case with so little time to prepare?

*You're not.*

"Tough break, Lexi."

*Squirrel*

I whip my head to the right and see Gregory standing there with a grin on his face. Rather than respond, I start to gather my things, ignoring the penetrating gaze of Squirrel.

"Maybe this thing doesn't have to drag out this long," Gregory says. "Meet me at my office in an hour. I'm sure we can come to an acceptable agreement regarding Mr. Kramer."

"Unless you're going to drop the charges, there's nothing to be agreed on," Squirrel seethes. His words are directed at Gregory, but his eyes never leave me.

"Let me handle this," I snap.

Before the conversation can go any further, a guard approaches the table to get Squirrel.

"I'm going to need a minute with him before you escort him back to the jail," I tell the guard.

"I have to get him back. You can come to the jail if you need to talk to him."

With that, the guard and Squirrel disappear.

"See you in an hour," Gregory says to my back.

I hear his footsteps retreating as I'm left to wonder just how much the chips are stacked against me, against *Squirrel*. All the while, I can feel the heat of unhappy, penetrating gazes of the other bikers in attendance.

Great. Just great.

I'VE BEEN SITTING HERE IN GREGORY FIRTH'S WAITING room for forty-seven minutes, not that I'm counting. He told me to meet him an hour after court, and it's been almost an hour and a half. I made a point to eat my lunch slowly, and I thought it was enough time. Apparently, my time doesn't matter to him.

I continue to skim Squirrel's file, unable to shake the feeling like something is... *off*. I can't pinpoint what it is, but the speed with which everything is moving is setting off alarm bells I've never heard before.

Lost in my concern, I don't hear the door open, and only take note of Gregory when he's standing in front of me, tapping his foot. When I look up at him, he smirks.

"I'm honestly surprised you showed up."

I adjust my glasses and tilt my head. "Why's that?"

Gregory shrugs. "Come on into my office."

He walks away, expecting me to follow, and I have no choice but to do that. After he shuts the door behind me, he gestures for me to sit in the chair next to his desk and takes his seat behind the mahogany monstrosity.

We sit there in silence for a moment, and Gregory stares at me as if contemplating how to begin. His expression is cocky, confident. I want to smack it off him.

"I see you came prepared," he says, nodding at the file in my hands.

"I'm always prepared."

"Good, that's good." Gregory leans forward and relaxes his shoulders like he's trying to put me at ease. It doesn't work. "But I'm afraid you're wasting your time. Mr. Kramer is guilty of murder, and no doubt a whole host of other felonies with that club of his. I'm prepared to offer him a plea deal in order to make it all go away."

My stomach drops at the same time my ears perk up. I was told to accept any plea deal that's offered, but so far, this stinks of rotting fish guts. First of all, if they truly believe Squirrel is guilty of murdering a fourteen-year-old girl, why would they be willing to simply dismiss that? And second, what else is up their sleeves? What other felonies do they plan on addressing and why haven't charges been filed?

"I'm listening," I finally say.

"Mr. Kramer pleads guilty to negligent homicide for the death of Maria Sampson and receives a sentence of two years in prison. He'll be out in one with good behavior."

"And the other felonies you mentioned?"

"The federal government is prepared to offer him immunity if he provides them with information on any and all Soulless Kings MC dealings. He cooperates with them, and he walks on everything he is involved in as a club member."

"If that's the case, why isn't the federal government here talking to me? Or why haven't they talked to him?"

Gregory heaves a sigh. "I have their authorization to offer the deal." His face is relaxed, but his tone has a bite to it.

Taken aback, I pretend to flip through my file while I think of something to say. I've never worked a case that involved the federal government, so in reality, I have no idea how it works with them. But I'd about bet the future of my career that this isn't it.

"Miss Cantor, can I be frank with you? Off the record?"

*Off the record? Not sure I like the sound of that.*

"Of course," I say instead. I don't know what drives me to do it, but I slip my hand into my pocket and pull out my cell phone. I glance at it before looking at Gregory with an apologetic smile. "I'm so sorry. My mother's sick, and she just texted me an update about her doctor's appointment this morning. Give me one sec."

He nods, completely oblivious to my lie. I take the time to make it seem like I'm responding to my mother when in fact, I'm setting my phone up to record the rest of the meeting. Call me crazy, but my gut tells me it's the right move.

After sliding my phone back into my pocket, careful not to press any buttons as I do, I smile at Gregory again.

"Sorry about that. It's been hard to keep up with her illness from this far away. Texting is the easiest and fastest way to stay in communication." I adjust in my chair and flap my hand as if to dismiss that line of conversation. "Anyway, you were saying you wanted to speak off the record."

"Yes. As long as you're in agreement that what is said off the record stays between us."

"Of course."

I allow myself to relax and for the next twenty minutes, I do nothing but listen to—and record—all the bullshit Gregory Firth spews.

# Chapter Four

*Fuck if I don't turn her on.*

### **Squirrel**

"Your attorney is here to see you."

I sit up on the cot in solitary and turn to face the door. I can see the guard's face, his brow raised, in the tiny window.

"C'mon, I don't have all day," he grumbles.

I rise and walk to the door, turning so my back is to it. The clanking of metal fills the space as the door is opened and cuffs are slapped on my wrists. I ignore the fact that they're too tight, knowing my comfort doesn't matter to these people.

I'm led back up to the first floor of the jail and toward the wing where inmate-attorney meetings take place. When we reach the door to the same room I was placed in earlier to meet with my attorney, I swipe my tongue over the dried blood on my lip and brace myself for having to give an explanation.

The guard opens the door and sits me down in the only empty chair. I can hear Miss Cantor's gasp when she sees me, but I don't make eye contact until we're alone.

"What the hell happened?" she demands as she stands and walks around the table.

"Nothing."

I wince when her delicate fingers touch the spot where my cheek is split open under my eye. She continues to poke and prod, moving from my face to the wounds on my arms. Before I know what's happening, her touch soothes the stinging pain, and I find myself soaking up the feeling.

*Fuck, she could touch me anywhere and light my body on fire.*

"Squirrel, this isn't *nothing*." She pulls her hands away and stands, staring me in the eyes the entire time. "What happened?"

"Drop it," I snap.

"No."

I narrow my eyes at her. "No?"

She shakes her head. "No."

"You've got balls, I'll give you that." I chuckle.

"I've got compassion. Big difference."

"Fine, compassion then," I concede. "The question is, why?"

"Why do I have compassion?" Confusion wrinkles her brow and flows into her words.

"Why do you have compassion for me?" When she doesn't immediately respond, I fill the silence. "Look, Miss Cantor, all I care about is getting the fuck out of here and clearing my name. If you can make that happen, great. But if not, tell me now so I can find a new lawyer."

"Lexi."

"What?"

*Squirrel*

"My name is Lexi. Miss Cantor is fine too, but if we're going to be spending as much time together as I think, you might as well call me Lexi."

"So you can get me out of here?"

"Honestly? I don't know." She returns to her chair and sits. "But I sure as hell am going to try."

There's something about a woman who can be honest, even when it might not work in her favor, that I gravitate toward. I don't like being lied to or led on. So her willingness to give me the truth is refreshing.

"Why?"

"Because it's my job." She swallows and, for a moment, I get lost in the slim column of her throat as it bobs. "And because I believe you're innocent."

"You do?"

Rather than answer, Miss Cantor—Lexi—reaches into her pocket and pulls her cell phone out. She sets it on the table and presses a button before leaning back in her chair.

Within seconds, a male voice comes through the speaker.

*"Good. Now, you know as well as I do, Mr. Kramer is a piece of shit, and the streets would be much safer without him."*

I recognize the prosecutor as the one speaking, and my entire body stiffens.

*"That being said, I couldn't care less about what happens to him. All I care about are numbers. Cases."*

There's a brief pause, as if he's waiting for whoever he's talking to say something.

*"Wins, Miss Cantor. I care about wins and money."*

*"Even if the defendant is innocent?"*

*"Look, it's not personal. I have a reputation to protect, a family to provide for. If that means a few low life's go to jail,*

*even for crimes they didn't commit, so be it. We both know that no one is really innocent."*

How is this guy allowed to practice law? He says I'm a piece of shit. Fine, I'll give him that. I'm not the most upstanding citizen, but I'm not a child killer. Nor am I someone who thrives on putting good people behind bars. Sure, I've killed before, but those people went before a judge and jury called the Soulless Kings MC. They were proven guilty. I haven't been proven guilty of anything, ever.

*"So what are you saying?"*

*"Convince Mr. Kramer to take the plea deals, and I'll make it worth your while."* He inhales. *"You said that your mother is sick. You can travel to help take care of her. You could take a vacation. Hell, you could do both and have money left over to pay your rent for several years. You won't regret it."*

*"And where is this money coming from?"*

At Lexi's question, I bristle and glare at her. She rolls her eyes at me, not seeming to care that she's ratcheting up my anger just as much as Gregory Firth at this point.

"Just listen," she prods.

*"Does it matter?"*

"No, I guess it doesn't."

*"Let's just say it's coming from someone who has a lot of it and the connections to match."*

"Mr. Firth, let me see if I understand this correctly. You want me to convince an innocent man to plead guilty and give his life up to the FBI because they want to build a case against his club? And you want this because someone, whom you refuse to name, is paying you to do so?"

*"That's one way to look at it, I suppose."*

"What other way is there?"

*"The right way,"* Gregory says with a condescending

tone. "We're both doing our jobs to the best of our ability. We'd be providing closure to the family of Maria Sampson, while also getting some pretty bad guys off the street. Sure, Mr. Kramer might not be guilty of this particular crime, but that doesn't mean he's a good guy. But with the immunity, he won't spend much time behind bars. What he will experience, which to me is punishment, is a disconnect from his club. And in that regard, aren't we doing him a favor? Besides, we'd be getting rich in the process. That is what we focus on."

I stand from my chair so fast, it topples over. "Is this guy for real?!"

"Just wait," Lexi says.

"Are you saying that you believe, or know, that Travis Kramer, a.k.a Squirrel, is innocent in the death of Maria Sampson?"

"Since we're off the record, yes, that's exactly what I'm saying. But you're still missing the bigger picture, Miss Can—"

Lexi stops the recording. As she leans back in her chair, a smile stretches her lips, and I can't help but think she's the most beautiful woman I've ever seen, even in the middle of this shit show.

"Okay, so we've established that the prosecutor is dirty," I finally say. "Now what?"

"First, I'm going to explain these plea deals to you because that's my job." She sits up straight and tugs a few papers out of one of her file folders. She slides them across the table toward me. "The first one is a plea deal for the charge of murder as relating to the death of Maria Sampson."

I lift the top page and begin to read as she talks.

"The state is willing to reduce the charge to negligent

homicide in exchange for a guilty plea. You'd be sentenced to two years in prison but would likely get out in one with good behavior."

"No, that's unacceptable. Next."

Lexi huffs out a breath. I don't know why she's so frustrated. This isn't her life and family on the line.

"The federal government is willing to offer you immunity in any and all charges relating to crimes committed with, and for, the motorcycle club, Soulless Kings."

"But they want my cooperation first?"

"Yes, they do. You would have to agree to be extensively interviewed by the FBI, as well as essentially become their confidential informant within the club. You'd be helping them to take down club members."

I shake my head in disbelief. "They really don't know MCs as much as they think, do they?"

"Excuse me?"

I toss the papers across the table at her. "The FBI. They don't know how clubs operate, do they?"

"I-I don't know."

Lexi uses her index finger to push her glasses up her nose. What I wouldn't give to be that finger, to be that close to her, even if she's beginning to infuriate me again.

"They really think I'm just going to roll over and take this deal? That I'm going to throw every last person in my family—because that's what we are, a family—under the bus and watch from my high horse as they rot in prison?" I chuckle humorlessly. "They're fucking nuts. And so are you if you think I'm going to agree to this."

"Squirrel, all I'm doing is laying out your options. I never once said I think you should do this."

"Then enlighten me. What is it you think I should do?"

That smile reappears but there's a slyness to it, a

devilish hint of something I wouldn't have attributed to her. "Off the record, I think you should tell them to fuck off and fight this to the bitter end." She shrugs as if that statement means nothing. "On the record, I can't tell you what to do, but in my professional opinion, you're innocent and should act accordingly."

"So don't take the deals?"

"Not what I said."

"Jesus, woman, you're confusing. Fucking spell it out for me."

Another sigh, this one laced with her own frustration. "We have this recording that proves this whole thing is rigged, based on a bribe. I can take this to the judge and have the charges dismissed. Of course, they'd likely be dismissed without prejudice which means you could be charged again. I think we hold onto the recording for a while, see how things play out. If we get to a point where we really need it, it'll be our ace in the hole."

"And in the meantime, what? I'm supposed to just sit in solitary for God knows how long because the other inmates, and guards, have already deemed me guilty for being a child killer?" I gesture toward my various injuries for emphasis. I never told her where they came from or why I got them, but this should suffice as an explanation.

"It'll be ninety days, max." She lets her gaze travel from my eyes, down to my chest and back again. "Surely someone like you can handle ninety days."

"Someone like me?"

Lexi's cheeks pinken, and I imagine they'd be warm to the touch. Fuck if I don't turn her on.

"Yeah, you know? Someone with your background, your... build."

"My build?" I taunt, savoring the way the corner of her

eye twitches when she's nervous, the way her cheeks darken with each passing second.

"Um..." Lexi licks her lips. "You're built, ya know? Strong. That's all I meant."

"Uh huh."

Lexi tries to collect herself, adjusting her glasses and her position, and it fascinates me. Something tells me there's a firecracker in there somewhere just waiting to explode past the nerdy, law-abiding package.

"I know this is frustrating, Squirrel," she says with a relative calm I don't think she really feels. "But I need you to trust me."

"Why should I trust you?" I counter. "I don't even know you."

Attraction does not equal trust. If I have my way, I'll get to explore both, but she doesn't need to know that.

"You should trust me because I'm the only one who truly believes you. I'm the only one who, in my gut, knows you didn't do this. And I know I can get you free from all of it."

"How?"

I like her confidence, but still don't know if there's really any basis for it or if she just wants to be right.

"By doing my job."

# Chapter Five

*I put my big girl panties on and resign myself for what is surely going to be the longest night of 'what ifs' in the history of forever.*

**Lexi**

Squirrel's begrudging 'fine' rings in my head as I walk into my office building. It's almost the end of the day, but I had to stop off and pick up a few more things so I can get some work done at home tonight. And all I can think of is that 'fine'.

"Hi Cheryl," I say to the receptionist at the entrance of the public defender's office.

"Oh, hey, Lexi," she says, rising from her chair. "I'm so sorry. I tried to stop them, but they insisted on seeing you and…" She looks toward my cubicle through the glass doors. "I tried, really I did."

I follow her gaze and see four bikers standing around my desk, crowding the small, gray cubicle. When I return my attention back to Cheryl, I give her a smile.

"It's okay." I rest my hand on top of hers. "Really, Cheryl. It's fine."

She nods but doesn't look convinced. Rather than waste my time consoling her, I walk through the doors toward the men. I hold my head up high, even though everything else in me has sunk to the floor, and close the distance between me and the uncertainty ahead.

"Gentlemen," I say as I try to get past them so I can set my stuff on my desk. "What can I do for you?"

"Is there somewhere private we can talk?"

I glance around the office and toward the meeting room. The blinds that cover the glass exterior of the space are open, so I can see that it's empty.

"Follow me."

I lead them to the meeting space and close the blinds after we all enter. I gesture for them to sit, but they hesitate.

"Is that thing on?" one says as he points to the recorder in the center of the table.

"Not unless you want it to be."

"No fucking way do we want it to be," another one says.

"Then, please, have a seat so we can get to the reason you're here."

The four of them take their time but eventually sit. Two on one side of me and two on the other. I don't know if they're intending to make me feel trapped, but if they are, they're succeeding.

"Sorry to come in here like this." The man reaches to shake my hand. "I'm Fender, President of the Oregon chapter of Soulless Kings MC and Squirrel's friend." I shake his hand before he gestures to the others. "This here is Joker, our Sergeant at Arms, Greaser, our Road Captain, and Flash, the club's Treasurer."

## Squirrel

"It's a pleasure to meet you all." I think. "I'm Lexi Cantor, Squirrel's attorney. But you already know that."

"Yeah, we do," Joker says. "And we're not real sure why you're his attorney. The club has an attorney."

*This goes deeper than I thought.*

"I think I know why."

I pull out my cell phone and play the same recording I played for Squirrel for them. The longer we listen, the more the air in the room thins. I thought Squirrel was intimidating, and he was in cuffs. These four are downright terrifying when they're angry.

"What the fuck is going on here?" Greaser demands. He stands and stabs a finger in my direction. "Are you in on this?"

"What?" I'm taken aback by the accusation. Did he not just listen to the same recording I did? "I'm not in on anything. I'm on Squirrel's side, on your side."

"And why should we believe you?" Fender asks, wariness in his tone.

"Because I'm telling the truth." It's a statement but comes out sounding more like a question.

"Not good enough," Joker snaps. "Answer the man's question."

I take a deep breath, trying to come up with the right words, the ones that will make them believe me.

"I am telling you the truth," I begin. When they all stiffen, I hold a hand up to stop any protests. "If you recall, nowhere on that tape did you hear me say I wanted the money or that I agreed to anything. Not only that, I advised Squirrel, who's *my* client by the way, not to accept the plea deals. I advised him to fight this. And I asked him to trust me, just like I'm asking you to."

"What did he say to that?" Flash asks.

"'Fine'. He said 'fine.'"

"Of course he said 'fine,'" Joker argues and then sweeps his hand toward me. "Look at her."

Fender holds up a hand. "Hold on a minute, J." He focuses his attention on the Sergeant at Arms. "Squirrel likes his women, but he's not a player like you. At least not when it matters so much. Give him the benefit of the doubt."

"This isn't about Squirrel," Joker contends. "This is about her."

"Now wait just a damn minute," I seethe, garnering their full attention and maybe even a look or two of respect. "If you think for one second this is about *anyone* other than Squirrel, you can march your ass right out of this office. Squirrel is the one with his life on the line here. He's the one who has to make an impossible decision. He's the *only* one who gets to question me or dictate how this case should be handled. Not me and certainly not you."

My chest heaves, although I'm not sure if it's from fear or excitement. Standing up to these men isn't high on my list of things I wanted to do today, but I realize someone has to stand up for Travis Kramer, the man, and not Squirrel, the club member.

"Wow," Fender says. "That was quite the speech."

I say nothing.

"If Squirrel is willing to trust you, then we're willing to do the same. But mark my words, Miss Cantor, betray him, or us, in any way, and this will be the last case you ever have."

I take in Fender's words, the brutal connotation to them, and nod. "Deal."

"Oh, that wasn't a deal," Greaser says. "It was a promise."

"He's right," Fender agrees. "But if a deal is what you're interested in..." He takes a piece of paper out of his vest pocket and slides it across the table to me. "... be at this address at six tomorrow morning."

"I have to work tomorrow," I protest, not bothering to look at the paper. "I can't just go gallivanting around at your—"

"We'll make sure you make it to work, Miss Cantor," Flash says. "You have our word."

If they think they were skeptical of me, they should be inside my brain right now. I don't trust any of them as far as I could throw them.

*Now you're starting to sound like Gregory. Don't go down that slippery slope.*

"May I ask what this meeting is about?"

"Yeah," Joker says. "You can ask. But the only answer you're getting is 'you'll see'."

With that, the men stand and start to exit the meeting room. Joker is the last one out the door, but he stops just across the threshold and shoots a look over his shoulder.

"Oh, and lose the suit. It'll only cause trouble."

He disappears with the others, and I'm left sitting alone, wondering what the hell I'm getting myself into. Maybe I should go to my boss and try to get myself thrown from the case. Maybe I shouldn't wait to take that recording to the judge. Maybe I should go back to the jail and meet with—

*No.*

Meeting with Squirrel again is definitely out of the question. My nerves and hormones can't take it.

Maybe. Maybe. Maybe.

There are too many to contemplate, so instead, I put my big girl panties on and resign myself for what is surely going to be the longest night of 'what ifs' in the history of forever.

## Chapter Six

*Fireworks. So many fucking fireworks.*

**Squirrel**

"Would you stop fucking pacing?"

I ignore Joker and continue to wear a path on the already worn floor of the shop. A quick glance at the clock has my stomach dropping even farther.

"She'll be here," Fender says in an effort to ease my frustration.

I stop in my tracks and turn to face him, as well as Joker, Greaser, Flash, and Sling, the president of our Michigan chapter. Our brothers are kind enough to let us use their Harley shop for this meeting. We discussed meeting at their clubhouse, but because of who Lexi is, or rather, what she is, they weren't quite comfortable with that.

"It's quarter after six. If she was going to be here, she'd be—"

## Squirrel

There's a pounding on the door, and all eyes turn toward it. Sling marches to the blue metal barrier and yanks it open. I can see his annoyance at her tardiness in the rigidity of his movements.

"You're late," Sling deadpans.

Lexi brushes past him, her head down. When she reaches the middle of the room, she lifts her chin and pushes her glasses up her nose. I'm instantly transported back to the moment she walked into the meeting room at the jail, the first time I saw her.

My earlier fear disappears, and I find myself staring at her, taking in the most amazing sight. She's wearing hip-hugging jeans, black and white Vans, and a long-sleeved tee with the Beatles on the front. It's such a one-eighty shift from the suit that it's mind-blowing. She's... perfect.

Lexi looks around at everyone until her eyes land on me, and a slight smile tugs at her lips.

"Sorry I'm late." She adjusts the bag slung over her shoulder, and I rush forward to take it from her.

"No problem," I assure her as I transfer the bag to my own shoulder.

"No problem?!" Sling bellows. "Not thirty seconds ago you were pacing around here like a caged animal about to explode. And now..." He throws his hands up in the air. "Now it's 'no problem'. What about the rest of us, huh? We all dragged our asses out of bed this morning, and her being late is the disrespect we get from—"

"Excuse me?" Lexi says quietly.

"What?" Sling asks as he faces her head on.

"I had to get up early too." Those damn glasses slide, and she slips them back into place. "I had to take care of Bug, and let me tell you, that's not easy to do when he doesn't want to get out of bed. Then I had to pack a bag so I had work clothes."

The longer she speaks, the louder she gets. Not to mention the way her shoulders are straightening and she's inching closer to Sling. "And then, your friend here..." She hitches a thumb over her shoulder at Fender. "... he failed to mention that I'd have a forty-five-minute drive to this, this..." She glances around her to finally take in the space. "... whatever the hell this is. So, I think you can cut me some slack for being a little late."

I stand there, waiting for Sling to read her the riot act. When his shoulders slouch and his face twists into a grin, I relax.

"I like you," Sling tells Lexi. "You've got balls. My only question is, are they big enough to handle what's coming?"

"That depends," she says. "What's coming?" Her brow furrows. "Wait." She turns to me. "First, what the hell are you doing here? You're supposed to be in solitary because you were denied bail."

Before I can answer, Fender speaks. "I think this is a good time to go into the office so we can sit and talk."

Lexi flaps her hand. "Works for me. This is your show, after all."

The others walk into the main area of the building, and Lexi and I follow. When she tries to keep up, I grab her arm and stop her. She looks between my hand and face, arching a brow.

"What are you doing?" she asks, clearly uncomfortable. The only thing to giveaway the other thoughts running through her mind is the way her cheeks darken.

I pull my hand away quickly, not wanting to overstep and scare her. "Look, I'm sorry about all of this."

"All of what?"

"Dammit, can't you just take the apology? Why do you always need more?"

That arched brow inches a little higher. "Always? We've known each other for a day, Mr. Kramer. I don't think you're in a position to judge how often I..." Lexi clears her throat. "... 'need more'."

"So we're back to Mr. Kramer now?"

For some reason, that bothers me more than the icicles dripping from her attitude. She and I were on an even keel until my brothers intervened. Don't get me wrong, I'm grateful they did, but shit. Where does that leave me as far as this woman is concerned?

"Until I know what this clandestine meeting is about, yes, we're back to that."

"Fine." I sweep an arm out toward the office. "After you."

Lexi rolls her eyes. She tries to hide the tiny smile, but I catch it just as she turns to walk away. I can't tell if she's enjoying this or just happy that she's still breathing around such 'pieces of shit'.

She enters the office before me, and the others are standing in there with impatient looks on their faces. I'm the one they glare at.

"Have a seat," Sling says, gesturing to one of the eight chairs situated around a round conference table.

In a moment of defiance, or stubbornness, Lexi walks around the table and takes a completely different seat. Sling huffs out a breath, but there's a chuckling quality to it and he's shaking his head.

The rest of us sit. Jealousy snakes through me when Joker and Sling take the chairs next to Lexi, leaving me to sit across from her. While I don't mind being able to look at her, I'd much rather sit close and feel her, even if it's from a few inches away.

Lexi nods in my direction but doesn't look at me. "How is he here?"

"First, let me introduce myself. I'm Sling." He shakes her hand. "President of the Michigan chapter of the Soulless Kings MC."

Lexi's eyes widen comically, but she quickly schools her features. "Lexi Cantor. Public defender of Mr. Kramer."

I grit my teeth at the name but say nothing.

"And that's what we're here to discuss," Fender says.

"Answer my question first, and then we can discuss my role."

"Ever hear the phrase 'money talks'?" Joker asks.

"Of course," Lexi scoffs. "I believe that's why Squir... I mean, Mr. Kramer, is in the position he's in."

Her slip up eases some of my frustration.

"Well," Joker begins. "Money talks."

"Care to elaborate?"

Fender huffs out a breath. "As a whole, Soulless Kings' have a lot of... assets. We quickly liquidated some of them, which allowed us to *encourage* the judge to see things differently in regard to Squirrel's bail."

"You bribed the judge?!" Lexi yells, shooting up from her chair.

"Sit down," Sling orders.

"No." Lexi crosses her arms over her chest, which effectively pushes her tits up making it easy to see the lace bra she's wearing.

"Like I said, balls."

Lexi adjusts her glasses and sits back down. She looks everywhere but at any of us. She's angry, and rightfully so, but if the club's plan is going to work, she's going to have to get over it, fast.

*Squirrel*

"Yes, we bribed the judge," Joker confirms and then under his breath says, "Among other things."

"I'm going to pretend I didn't hear that."

"Whatever helps you sleep at night, Balls." Sling chuckles. "Bottom line is everyone has a price and Judge Belmont's is half a mil and a promise to keep her kiddos out of it. Didn't care as much about her husband though."

"Again, pretending I didn't hear that," Lexi repeats.

Fender reaches into his cut and pulls out a bulky envelope, sliding it on the table toward Lexi.

She looks at it, her eyes narrow. "What's that?"

"Money," Fender says simply. "And a lot of it."

Lexi snaps her head up and glares at Fender. "If you think I'm going to take a bribe, you're sa—"

"It's not a bribe," I bark, releasing some of the pent-up frustration with her, and all of them. They're scaring her away and none of its necessary. Or at least I don't think it is.

Finally, she locks eyes with me. "Then what is it?"

"It's money, like Fender said. But to pay you, not bribe you."

"I fail to see the difference, Mr. Kramer." The bite in her tone irks me.

"The difference, Lexi," Flash says, chiming in for the first time since her arrival. "Is that we're offering to pay you for a service, not bribe or threaten you."

Lexi relaxes in her chair slightly. She's still on guard, but it's waning.

"I'm listening."

She focuses on Flash. Maybe because he comes across as less threatening, maybe it's simply because he's the last one who spoke to her. Either way, it pisses me off because I want her attention.

Flash clears his throat as he pulls a folded-up contract

out of his inside cut pocket. He hands it to her. "This outlines everything, for legal purposes, but essentially, we want to hire you to be Squirrel's attorney."

"I'm already his attorney."

"Yes, but as a member of the public defender's office," Fender qualifies. "We'd like you to represent Squirrel alongside the Soulless Kings' attorney, Alan Forney."

"No," I say.

"What?" Fender growls, turning toward me. "We discussed this."

"I know we did," I agree. "And I'm on board. But I want Lexi to be the attorney of record. I want her taking the lead."

"That's not what we agreed on," Fender reminds me.

"Trust me, I know. But I had all night to think about it, and it's what I want."

"Why?" Lexi asks me.

"Exactly," Joker says. "Why? She's inexperienced, timid in court, annoying as—"

"And she believes in me." I scan the room. "Lexi believes in me. And while you're not wrong on all counts, she's also confident, smart, and has, as Sling put it, balls. She leads this thing, or I'm out."

Before Fender, or anyone else, can argue, Lexi interjects. "Even if all those things weren't a factor, it's the only choice you have. Unless this Forney guy is licensed to practice law in Michigan."

I glance at Fender, and it's clear by his blank expression that he doesn't know if Alan is or not. No matter. I'm serious when I say it's her or nothing.

"Fine," Fender finally says. "But if she fucks this up and you land your ass back in jail, you're the only one you can point the finger of blame at."

## *Squirrel*

"I won't fuck it up," Lexi says quickly.

"So, Balls, you're in?" Sling asks, his brow raised at her.

"Well, no, I didn't say that."

"Jesus, you're a pain in the ass," Joker grumbles. "You take us around in circles, questioning everything, and still string us along. Either you're in or you're out. It's not a hard decision."

"You better get used to me questioning everything, if we're going to work together." Lexi reaches to pull the envelope toward her, but she doesn't open it. "Questioning things is my job. It's what got us to this point." She takes a deep breath and continues. "You realize if I do this, I'll have to quit my job at the public defender's office, right? Because there's no way I'll be able to go against orders without getting fired anyway. What's in it for me, beyond money, if I do this? I can't just give up my career for one case."

"For starters, you'll be helping an innocent man," I snap, unjustifiably angry that she's not willing to do this for me, no questions asked. "Not to mention the guilty motherfuckers acting on a bribe… you'll ruin their careers."

"Okay, but I can do that by simply taking my recording to the judge, right?"

"Sure, but then you won't get to see how this plays out."

"And how is this going to play out?" she asks, finally getting to the heart of the matter.

"We take 'em all out," Fender states. "One by one, we ruin each and every individual who is a part of this, until we reach the puppet master. And then we burn his world to the ground."

"Do it right," Flash adds. "And there will be huge career implications for you at the end. Who knows?" He shrugs. "There just might be a position in Oregon as an attorney for a certain MC."

I watch Lexi as she considers this. She might come across as slightly nerdy and obsessively law-abiding, but there are other sides to her. A side which wears Beatles tees and Vans. A side which stands up for what's right. A side which knows that sometimes you have to do the scary thing in order to accomplish the right thing.

A ballsy side.

A wild side.

A sexy as fuck side.

And I want to explore them all. That's why, when I think about the possibilities if she says yes, fireworks shoot off inside of me.

Lexi lifts the envelope, counts the money, and shoves it in her bag.

"I'm in," she says.

Fireworks.

So many fucking fireworks.

# Chapter Seven

*I'm drawn to him, more than I should be.*

**Lexi**

I take deep breaths and stare at my cell. Bug is curled up next to me, on the couch, and his snoring offers me comfort. Unfortunately, it's not enough for the phone call I have to make. I stab a finger at the contact name and lift the phone to my ear.

"Hello?"

One last deep breath. "Hi Mom."

"Oh," she says, and I can practically feel her disdain through the phone. "Hi, Lex."

"Are you busy? Is Dad home?"

"I'm always busy, but you wouldn't know that because you never come visit. And yes, your father is home."

"Mom, I've only been gone for ten months, not years on end," I remind her, even though it's pointless. "Can you get Dad and put the phone on speaker? I've, um…" I swallow past the lump in my throat. "I've got some news."

Mom puts me on hold while she gets my dad. I take the time to review what I plan to say. It's not much, that's for sure. As part of the deal with the Soulless Kings, I can't tell anyone exactly what's going on other than I quit my job at the public defender's office to take on another case. And I won't even get into how Joseph Hinton took the news. If he's any indication, I'm going to go down in a blaze of false glory.

"Lexi, honey, how are you?" my dad asks when they get back on the line.

"Hi Dad. I'm good."

"Your mom says you've got news."

"I do." Bug yips in his sleep, and I rub his neck. Here goes nothing. "I, um, well, I quit my job at the public defender's office."

"Oh, honey," Mom cries, clearly thrilled with the news. Her complete shift in attitude is not lost on me. Nor does it matter because it won't last. "That's wonderful. What firm did you take a position with? One here near the Bronx, I hope."

"I'm not going to be working with a firm, Mom."

"But... what does this mean?" Mom asks wearily.

"Are you moving home?" Dad asks.

"No, Dad, I'm not moving home." I leave out the part where all of this may culminate in me moving to Oregon and instead focus on what I can tell them right now. "And I didn't take a job with a firm, Mom. But I will be working as a lawyer... on my own. I've decided to give hanging out my own shingle a shot."

"How could you do this?!" Mom screeches. "You know we count on the money you send, even if it's very little."

The derision in her voice burns through me like acid. "I'm aware."

"Oh, don't get so uptight Lexi Lynn," Dad instructs.

The acid burns through all my filters, and I crack. "Uptight? How am I being uptight, Dad? I've sent you what money I could while only leaving myself enough to survive on. You both have this image of me living the high life of an attorney. I have news for you! I was doing better when I was living under your roof in the Bronx."

As the anger gives way to tears, I swipe at my cheeks. After a few hiccupping breaths, I compose myself.

"Instead of having unrealistic expectations for me, why don't you try being happy for me? I'm excited about this." For reasons still unknown. Okay, I know what the reason is, but I'm sure as hell not telling my parents about Squirrel. They'd have me committed. "I'm sorry I'm such a failure in your eyes."

Without waiting for any response, I disconnect the call and throw my phone onto the couch on the other side of Bug. When the device bounces off the cushion and hits the floor, he lifts his head and gives me a sloppy kiss.

I lean in and wrap my arms around him. "You still love me, don't ya Bug?"

Tears slide down my cheeks, and Bug tries to lick them away. When that only results in my face becoming slobbery, I let out a laugh and silently thank whatever force is out there for bringing this sweet dog into my life. I don't know what I'd do without him.

I brush the last of my tears away and make a decision: I'm not going to let my parents' inability to accept my life choices diminish my excitement about what's to come. Maybe I'm fooling myself and this will turn into the worst thing I've ever done. Who knows?

What I do know is I can't predict the future, so I might as well enjoy the ride. With that in mind, I go to the kitchen,

Bug on my heels, and pour myself the last little bit of boxed wine I have in the fridge and carry it to the bathroom.

I draw a bath, dumping in a generous amount of the cheap bubble bath sitting on the edge. I strip off my clothes and climb in, letting the warm water ease my stress.

As I soak in bliss, I can't help but think about the money stashed in the bottom drawer of my dresser. When I counted the money before leaving the meeting with the Soulless Kings, it was all I could do not to react. Two hundred and fifty thousand dollars. That's what I have sitting in this rinky dink apartment right now.

*What I could do with that kind of money.*

Exactly! There are so many things. I glance around the tiny bathroom, the cream tub surround, and realize the first thing I need to do is find a new place to live. Something bigger, something safer, something more... everything.

I'll do what I've always done and send my parents some of the money, but not all of it, and certainly not what they expect. Five thousand should hold them over for a while.

Seeing as there was no discussion on whether or not that would be my only payment, and if not, when the next one would come, I don't want to go crazy. I'll start with new living arrangements and my parents and go from there.

I don't know how long I stay in the tub, coming up with a plan to go apartment—or house, condo... whatever I want —hunting tomorrow, after my next meeting with the club, but when I pull myself back to the present, the water is cool. I drain the rest of my wine and the bath water before climbing out and wrapping myself in a towel.

Walking through each room, I make sure all the lights are off and the front door is locked. I grab my cell and head to bed. It's been a long day and tomorrow is shaping up to be just as long.

*Squirrel*

After throwing on a pair of soft pink sleep shorts and shirt, I crawl under the covers and then press the side button to wake my cell and see several missed calls, as well as texts, from my parents. I scroll through the messages. My mom chastises me for hanging up on them and my dad apologizes for how they reacted. Both of them continue to question my decision.

I decide not to respond. It wouldn't do me any good anyway, so what's the point? Moving on from their negativity, I open up social media and locate the Soulless Kings' Facebook page. I look through all the pictures, again, finding the ones that include Squirrel. I'm drawn to him, more than I should be. He's a client, nothing more.

Unfortunately, my subconscious doesn't understand boundaries and my dreams are filled with him.

Not that I'm complaining.

# Chapter Eight

*She's my target and being pulled toward any other landing spot is unacceptable.*

**Squirrel**

"You're nuts."

I heave a sigh for what feels like the millionth time since the beginning of this conversation. Alan Forney is a phenomenal attorney, and there's no denying his history with the Soulless Kings, but he's not right for this job. I feel it in my gut. Too bad he doesn't.

"Maybe I am," I concede, done arguing with him. "But it's my life, my decision."

"Fender, talk some damn sense into the boy," Alan demands. "I've been the club's attorney for years, and no one will do a better job representing him than I will. Shit, it's why you pay me the big bucks."

Fender, who's sitting calmly at the table while I pace the small space, holds up a finger at me when I open my mouth to argue.

## Squirrel

"Alan, do you really think I haven't tried?" Fender counters. "He's not budging on this one."

"You're his goddamn president!" Alan shouts so loud that if he were in the room with us and not on speaker phone, the windows would have rattled.

"And your employer," Fender growls. "You better remember where all the money for your hifalutin shit came from, Alan. It'd be a shame if one day that all disappeared."

"Are you threatening me?"

"Fuck no." Fender chuckles and while it sounds like there's humor in it, only those who know him well know it contains exactly what Alan is accusing him of... threat. "I'm simply reminding you who pays your bills. Don't get me wrong, the market for shady lawyers is massive, but you'd be hard pressed to find a job that pays as well with as little actual work as you do."

Silence comes through the line, so long I wonder if I missed the part where Alan hung up. But then he speaks, and his tone is full of resignation.

"Fine," he huffs. "Squirrel, if you want to throw your life away, that's none of my business. And, as requested, I'll assist this, this... lady lawyer. But remember, I offered a better way."

Everything in me screams to take the win, to end the call and be grateful Alan quit putting up a fight. But is that what I do? Not even close. The bigger part of me needs to drive home that he's not in charge and not the best person for this job.

"Let me ask you something, Alan," I say.

"Shoot."

"Are you a licensed attorney?"

"Of course I am. You know that."

"What states are you licensed in?"

"Fender, is this really necessary?" Alan asks rather than answer my question.

"If Squirrel thinks it is, then yes."

"Oregon," Alan grits out. "I'm licensed in Oregon."

"But the trial will be in Michigan. Can you practice law in Michigan?"

"As a matter of fact, yes." Alan's tone holds a hint of victory. And I get it, he thinks he's won and that I'm some idiot. Problem for him is, I'm not. "Michigan has reciprocity for Oregon. And every single other state for that matter."

"You're right, it does. But you have to establish residency with your practice in Michigan. You have to have an office, one where the phone is answered during business hours, mail can be sent to. Ya know...business stuff. How do you plan on doing that?"

"I'd get an office."

"And who would finance that office?"

Alan takes a deep breath and air whooshes from his lungs. "The Soulless Kings would."

"Wait just a damn minute," Fender interjects. "What in the hell makes you assume that?"

"Because that's how this partnership works," Alan says hotly. He's dangerously close to crossing a line and he's a fool if he doesn't know it. "I'm here for all your legal needs and you handle whatever is required so I can do that."

"That's just it, Alan," I say, stepping in before Fender fires him on the spot. Not that it matters considering we now have Lexi... sort of. "Why would we pay to have an office set up for you when we already have an attorney here? One who requires much less financially to get the job done?"

"I, I... well, I guess you wouldn't."

"Exactly." I finally sit and lean close to the cellphone in

the middle of the table. "*That* is why Lexi is better for this job. She thinks things through. She doesn't leap at the chance of a payday. She follows her gut and does what she thinks is right. Not just because she's paid by us, but because it's how she's built. She's representing me *despite* what it could do to her career, not because of the money she's making."

"Now, Squirrel, that's not fair," Alan protests. "I've always done great work for the club, and this would be no—

"You have," I agree. "But we're doing things differently for this one. Either you're on board or you're not. Which is it?"

"Fender, since when do you sit back and let your subordinates call the shots?"

"First of all," Fender seethes. "We're a family. Yes, they are technically my subordinates, but do you really think I'd sit back and let them call the shots if I didn't agree with them?" Fender pauses but not long enough for Alan to respond. "Secondly, Squirrel—and every other Soulless King for that matter—is as much your boss as I am. So, I suggest you answer his fucking question."

I fully expect Alan to continue to fight this, so when he doesn't, I'm surprised. "I'm on board."

"Good. I'll have Lexi call you so you two can coordinate. She will be given a lump sum of money to be used for trial expenses or any way she sees fit. That includes arrangements for you to be here." I grin, knowing Alan is likely fuming on the other end of the line. "I suggest you make nice with her."

"Fine," Alan says from between what I assume are clenched teeth. "I look forward to hearing from her."

Fender's grin spreads almost as wide as mine. "I'm sure

you do." With that, he disconnects the call and shifts so he's facing me fully. "That was fun."

"Your definition of fun is seriously warped, you know that, right?"

"Of course I do." Fender chuckles and this time there's humor in it. A lot of humor. "How the hell do you think I put up with you fucks so well?"

"Jesus," I mumble but my humor matches his. I run my fingers through my hair and heave a sigh. "I need a damn drink. And a toke. What about you?"

"Like I said... fun."

Fender gets up and walks out of the room the Michigan chapter provided us for that phone call. I follow him, and when we're greeted in the main area of the clubhouse, I engage with others as they call out.

"There he is," Sling yells over the music. "So, how'd the prick take it?"

"Fucker's on board," I reply.

I reach the bar and wait for a beer to be set in front of me. I've learned in the twenty-four hours I've been here, they do things a bit differently. You don't choose what you want to drink. The bartender, Courtney, seems to know what you'd like, and so far, she's always right.

A local IPA is what I'm given, and I take a long pull from the bottle. "Damn, Courtney, this is good."

She winks at me. "I know."

I let out a chuckle as my eyes stray to the skin peeking out over the top of her shirt. I don't let my gaze remain there for long but not because she's not appealing. Courtney absolutely is, and normally, I'd be trying to work an angle to get her into bed. But not now. Not after meeting Lexi.

It takes three more drinks and a joint to let my thoughts about Lexi settle into some form of acceptance.

## Squirrel

Lexi is different. I've only seen her three times, but from the moment she barreled through the door, late and disheveled, I was hooked. There's something about her that sucks me in, like the ground to a skydiver.

She's my target and being pulled toward any other landing spot is unacceptable.

# Chapter Nine

*While it feels wrong after the fact, it felt so damn right in the moment.*

**Lexi**

"Here Comes the Sun" by The Beatles pulls me from one hell of a dream. I silently say 'goodbye' to Squirrel and crawl out of bed. The further I can distance myself from my subconscious, the better.

I flip through the clothes in my closet and try to come up with something appropriate to wear. I don't have much beyond suits, at least that I feel comfortable conducting business in, but the Soulless Kings made it clear that any meetings with them would be casual. Sure, it's serious stuff we're dealing with, but that doesn't seem to matter to them.

Unsatisfied with my hanging wardrobe, I shift to my dresser. I come up with a pair of jeans and a short-sleeved tee. I can wear a suit jacket over it and feel like I'm not totally caving in my beliefs about what constitutes work attire.

## Squirrel

Before I can grab a shower, Bug races from the bedroom to the living room and back again. I detour to where his leash hangs so I can take him out to do his morning business. I throw on the hoodie I have hanging by the door and hook Bug up.

It takes a minute to unlock the deadbolt because the thing is so old and rusty, and once it's free, I swing open the door and stop dead in my tracks. Bug starts barking incessantly, pulling on his leash to get to the man standing there with his fist raised like he was about to knock.

"What are you doing here?" I demand, not really upset but completely thrown off balance by his presence.

"Good morning to you too," Squirrel says, his voice low and smooth. He squats so he's eye level with Bug and reaches out to scratch his ears. "And who's this?"

Bug, the asshole, slinks to his belly and allows Squirrel to love on him. He's not just an asshole, he's a *traitorous* asshole.

"Bug, up," I command, and he does what he's told. "Sit." Bug wiggles his butt but listens. I lift my eyes to Squirrel, who is now standing tall and towering over me. "That's Bug."

"Yeah, kinda figured when you were calling him that."

Squirrel chuckles and it scratches my nerves like fingernails on a chalkboard. It's too early for this shit.

I lower my head, trying to regain my composure, and my breath hitches when I catch sight of what I'm wearing. Well, shit.

"Don't worry about how you look," Squirrel says quietly. "You look cute." He shrugs. "Shit, you could wear a giant paper bag and you'd look great."

My head whips up so fast it makes my neck hurt. Heat rises in my cheeks, and my palms sweat.

*Cute? He thinks I'm cute?*

I clear my throat and attempt to coat my mouth with saliva. I don't know whether to be thrilled that he seems to like how I look or annoyed at the fact that he said 'cute' and not 'sexy'. Either way, I'm uncomfortable with compliments and hate that it shows.

"Why are you here?" I ask again in an effort to move past the awkwardness.

Squirrel narrows his eyes at me as if trying to determine if he crossed a line "Right. Well, we have a meeting this morning, and I came to give you a ride."

"I don't need a ride. I have a car," I remind him, pointing past him toward the parking lot.

He throws a quick glance over his shoulder and laughs. "That thing?" I nod. "That's not a car, it's a beat-up cage that's seen better days."

"Better days or not, it's mine and it gets me from point A to point B."

"And now you can afford to get something new."

"Is that right?" I sneer. It's his turn to nod, and when he does, my shoulders stiffen. "Money doesn't last forever. You know that, right?"

"I do."

"Good. Then you must know that I plan to spend the money the club gave me wisely. Not throw it away on frivolous things."

"Okay," he says hesitantly. "Then what do you plan on spending it on?"

"None of your business," I snap before looking down at Bug. "Come." I tug on his leash and brush past Squirrel. "If you'll excuse me, I have to walk my dog. I'll see you at the clubhouse."

"I'll wait."

*Squirrel*

I stop in my tracks at his words, but only for a split second. I lead Bug toward the pitiful dog area the apartment complex has and wait while he finds just the right spot to pee. It's another ten minutes before he finishes, and we head back to the apartment.

When my front door comes into view, I breathe a sigh of relief because it's closed. Good, Squirrel left. A quick glance around the parking lot doesn't reveal a Harley or any vehicles I don't recognize. A flash of sadness hits me because, if I'm being honest, there's a small part of me, way deep down, that wishes he'd have stayed.

But he didn't, and that's better.

I push open the door with the intent on going straight to the shower. My hand flies to my throat, and I gasp when I see Squirrel going through my albums. He slowly looks at me, as if it's no big deal that he invited himself in.

"Jesus, you scared me," I chastise.

"Sorry," he mumbles. "Figured you'd know I was in here. I told you I was going to wait."

Rolling my eyes, I disconnect the leash from Bug. When he runs straight to Squirrel for more ear scratches and belly rubs, annoyance races through my veins.

"If you don't mind, I've got things to do." Squirrel simply stares at me. "Alone, Squirrel. I've got things to do that don't require your presence."

He shrugs. "Don't let me stop you."

A groan escapes and I stomp toward the bedroom. "Sit down and don't touch anything. I'll be quick."

Bug sits but Squirrel remains in place. I slam the bedroom door behind me and lean against it. Inhaling deeply, I fill my lungs and count to ten. I do this for several minutes in an effort to ground myself. Squirrel's presence threw me for a loop I wasn't expecting this morning, and I feel completely unprepared.

As I make my way to the shower, I strip my clothes off and let them fall to the floor. I feel more exposed with Squirrel in my apartment. There's a flicker of something else, something... exciting.

"Get a grip," I mumble under my breath.

I turn on the shower and wait for the water to warm up before stepping into the tub. As the heat penetrates my muscles, I find myself relaxing and letting my mind wander.

I'm naked. And Squirrel is here. Against my better judgment, I allow my dreams to take over and am immediately flung back into a state of bliss.

I try to ignore the feelings as I wash my hair, but when they're still there after I'm done, I give into temptation. I snag the vibrator from the wall cubby and turn it on. The buzzing ramps up my desire, and I close my eyes as I slide the pink toy to my clit.

A moan bursts from me, and I clamp my mouth closed, not wanting Squirrel to hear me. That would be disastrous.

Using my free hand, I glide a finger through my folds before shoving it into my pussy. The combination of penetration and intense vibrations yanks me to the edge. I picture Squirrel kneeling in front of me, replacing my finger with his tongue. He laps at me, drinking up my arousal.

Every muscle in my body tenses as I fall over the edge of the cliff. I groan out my release, no longer able to control the noise level.

As I try and climb back out of the oblivion, shame washes over me.

*What the hell did I just do?*

Not only did I use fantasies about a client to get off, but

*Squirrel*

said client is in the other room. I've reached a new low. Or a new high. I guess that depends on how you look at it.

I fling open the shower curtain and wrap myself in a towel. I take my time getting dressed and ready to go. Squirrel's deep voice flows into the bedroom, and it sounds like he's talking to Bug. It's hard to tell though, with the muffling the door provides.

Before I open the door, I square my shoulders and put my shower out of my mind. I have nothing to be ashamed of, especially because Squirrel doesn't know what I did.

And while it feels wrong after the fact, it felt so damn right in the moment.

# Chapter Ten

*It's sudden and unexpected but anger barrels through me like a tornado tearing through an unsuspecting town.*

**Squirrel**

"And she has great taste in music."

I hold up an AC/DC album to show Bug. I've spent the last few minutes talking to him like he understands me. When his head tilts, I can't help but wonder if he does.

"Tell me, Bug, does she have a—"

Noise coming from the bedroom has me tilting my head like Bug to listen. I step up to the door and press my ear against it. Silence greets me for several seconds until the noise fills the air again.

"Holy shit," I whisper and glance at Bug. "Your master is having one hell of a shower."

Bug's head tilts from side to side, and I can't help but laugh. The moaning on the other side of the door increases. My cock grows painful against my zipper, so I reach down to adjust myself. If I knew for sure how much longer she'd be, I'd jack off right here, right now.

A loud bang reaches my ears, and my lips pull up into a grin when I realize she must be pounding on the shower wall. Oh, she's close, if not already teetering that ledge.

I close my eyes and picture Lexi bringing herself to that place of unfettered bliss, that place that a man should be bringing her to. And not just any man. No. *I* should be taking her there, and so many other places.

"You're killing me," I say through gritted teeth.

The sexy moans die down until silence washes over me. I force my thoughts to something else, anything else.

*You're fighting a murder charge.*

Yeah, that does it. My erection dwindles—too slowly but it's better than nothing—and when I hear her footsteps in the bedroom, I'm grateful. If things would have continued, even for a few more seconds, I'd have to explain why my pants were damp. I can hear it now: 'Oh, that. I just exploded like a randy fucking teenager seeing his first pair of tits.'

I walk to the couch and sit down to wait not so patiently for Lexi to finish up. It doesn't take long and when she steps through the doorway, my dick springs back to life.

Clad in jeans that hug her curves like a junkie holds a needle and a temptingly tight white tee under a black cropped suit jacket, Lexi is… stunning. Even as she pushes up the glasses resting on her nose, I find it harder and harder to stop myself from reaching out and helping, just for a chance at touching her.

"Feel better?" I ask without standing up.

Her eyes lock onto mine and she blushes. She quickly masks her embarrassment but not before the rush of satisfaction rushes through me at knowing what she was doing.

Shy, buttoned-up attorney has a side of her I bet she rarely lets out.

I vow then and there to tease that side of her out, as much as possible. Might as well start now.

A few minutes pass while Lexi gathers her laptop, some files, and shoves them in a bag. She also takes the time to make sure Bug's food and water bowls are full. I glance at the old clock on the wall and see we still have plenty of time before the meeting at the clubhouse starts.

"Hey, you hungry?" I ask her.

Her forehead crinkles for a moment, like she's trying to figure out the right answer, not that there is one.

"I, uh..." Lexi clears her throat. "I usually just eat a granola bar or something on my way to the office."

"That still doesn't answer my question."

She worries her bottom lip between her teeth and nudges her glasses up, looking around everywhere but at me. "Oh, um, no." She shakes her head. "I'm not hungry."

I eye her skeptically but decide to let it go. She's not going to make this easy, that's for sure.

"Okay. Then we should probably get going." We have time, but I can't be cooped up with her in this apartment longer than I have to. My libido can't take it.

"You go ahead and go," Lexi says. "I'll be right behind you."

"No."

Finally, her eyes dart to mine and she raises a brow. Fuck, she's sexy.

"No?"

"We'll go together."

"I don't think so."

"It's not a request," I tell her, hoping it'll end Lexi's defiance.

## Squirrel

I was so wrong.

Her eyes flash fire, and my skin burns where her searing gaze touches. She abandons whatever it is she's fiddling with in the kitchen and steps around the peninsula to close the distance between us.

"Listen up, *Mr.* Kramer." Lexi stabs a finger into my chest. "You're my client, not my caretaker." She squares her shoulders, and as much as I'd rather jump to the part where she gives in, I'm enjoying this little display of rebellion. "Furthermore, your club has paid me to do a job, not to be at their beck and call."

It's sudden and unexpected, but anger barrels through me like a tornado tearing through an unsuspecting town.

"That's where you're wrong," I growl, leaning down to be at eye level with her. "While you work for the Soulless Kings MC, we own you. You're right that I'm not your caretaker, but I am your boss—at least one of them—and you'll do what I say."

Lexi's shoulders slump as she lowers her eyes but not before I see the hurt in the sparkle of fresh tears. Dammit, this is not how I wanted this to go. She takes a step back and remains silent for a few seconds before lifting her head.

She takes a deep breath and exhales. "Fine. But we're taking my car. I've got shit to do afterward... alone."

Sensing this is as close to what I want as I'm going to get, I nod.

"Good. Let's go then."

∼

"What took you so fucking long?"

I glance at Lexi, who's to my left and slightly behind me, before returning my attention to Flash.

"Nothing."

"Somehow I doubt that," he drawls.

"Doubt all you want," I tell him. "Where is everybody?" I look around the clubhouse, and it's empty, other than a few passed out brothers with whatever Bangin' Betty they shared their night with. "We should get this meeting going."

"Not so fast." Flash steps up to me, a scowl on his face. "I had to wait for my goddamn breakfast because of you. Sling's Ol' Lady, Steph, made a practical feast, and Sling wouldn't let anyone touch it until you two got here."

"Fine. Where is it?"

"It's in their meeting room. Since we have a special guest," he nods at Lexi. "Sling relaxed the rules about who's allowed in that room. But only for breakfast."

Lexi finally steps around me and smiles at Flash. "That sounds wonderful, and I appreciate everyone thinking of me."

Flash grins back at her. "You hungry, Darlin'?"

I flex my hands, itching to lay him out on the floor. I assumed by insisting that Lexi handle my case that I'd marked my territory, but apparently not. I mentally add that to my list of things to do.

Lexi's eyes lift to mine before she returns her attention to Flash. "Actually, I am hungry."

"Are you fucking kidding me?" I bark.

"Damn, bro, chill out," Flash instructs.

I take a few deep breaths to get my temper under control. It works, barely, and I force a smile at Lexi.

"If you're hungry, then let's go eat."

She pushes those infernal glasses up her nose and gives me a half smile. "Sounds good."

Lexi and I follow Flash to the kitchen where the others are waiting.

## Squirrel

"Finally," Joker grumbles. "I'm starving and apparently, this chapter has manners and shit."

"We have manners," Fender states. "They just fly out the window when we're starving."

"I'm sorry for the wait." Lexi takes the empty seat around the island. "We would've been here sooner if Squirrel hadn't been so... difficult."

"Way to go Squirrel." Greaser chuckles. "Piss off your attorney before she really gets started."

"I didn't piss her off," I insist, annoyed that they're all ganging up on me.

"Let's table business for the moment." Sling slides up to the island with a plate in his hand. "I'm too hungry to deal with that shit now."

"Sounds good to me," Flash agrees.

"Me too," Lexi says and then she hops off the stool. "First, could someone show me where the bathroom is?"

"I've got ya, hun." Steph steps through the door at just the right moment. "Come with me."

The two ladies exit the room, and I jump at the chance to set the records straight on Lexi.

"You can all back the fuck off where Lexi is concerned," I say, louder than necessary in the small space.

"Is that right?" Fender asks, his expression a cross between pissed at the demand and thrilled at the admission coming.

"Yes, that's right." I nod. "She's mine, in case you haven't figured that out yet." I glare at Flash. "And apparently some of you haven't."

Flash holds his hands up. "I hear ya loud and clear brother. She's off limits."

"Any questions?" I ask and glance around at everybody.

A chorus of 'no's fill the air with a few chuckles mixed in.

"Wait," Fender says. "I do have one question."

"What?"

"Is Lexi aware that she's been claimed?"

A growl barrels out of my chest.

"Not yet. But she will."

## Chapter Eleven

*Maybe Squirrel is right. But I'll be damned if I'm going to tell him that.*

**Lexi**

"So, Miss Cantor, what do you think?"

I stare out the large window overlooking the downtown area, taking in the tall buildings and imagining all the lights lit up at night. The penthouse apartment is a far cry from the shit hole I'm in now.

"I'll take it."

"No, she won't."

I twist to glare at Squirrel, who, for reasons beyond me, insisted he be a part of this home hunt. I considered arguing with him about it, but there was something about the look in his eyes at the time that stopped me. I couldn't put my finger on it, but it seemed a lot like... possession.

"And why won't she?" I tap my foot in irritation.

"Because the building isn't secure," Squirrel says matter-of-factly. "This is the third place this man has shown us, and none of them are secure enough."

"For who? Me, or you?"

Squirrel lifts a shoulder. "Both." It comes out sounding more like a question. He turns to the realtor and asks, "Do you have any houses for rent, something away from the city, with minimal neighbors?"

The realtor scrolls through his phone clumsily and almost drops the papers full of the specs for the places he's shown me already. Finally, he lifts his head and gives a lopsided grin.

"Actually, I think I have just the thing." He turns his cell phone for Squirrel to see. "It's a ranch house on an acre of land, two bedrooms, one and a half baths and a fully finished basement with an office space. It's about a ten-minute drive from the city, and there are no immediately adjacent neighbors."

"Now wait just a damn minute." Crossing my arms over my chest, I scowl. "I'm your client, Mr. Bunyon, not him." I stab a finger in Squirrel's direction. "I would appreciate it if you would stop acting as if I'm some stupid woman who can't make decisions for herself."

"I'm sorry, I just thought..." His eyes shift from mine to Squirrel and back again. "It won't happen again."

I ignore the part where he failed to mention what he thought and relax my stance. "Thank you. Now, can I see that listing?"

"Of course." Mr. Bunyon turns the cell so I can look.

The more pictures I scroll through, the more excited I get. The house is perfect. It's updated, has plenty of space, and a yard for Bug to play in.

"What about pets?"

The realtor skims through the listing again and grins. "It says they allow pets for an additional monthly fee."

I look at the pictures again and am careful to school my

*Squirrel*

expression so Squirrel can't see the anticipation. I like this house. It fits all my requirements, and the rent is affordable. Not that that matters much anymore.

During the meeting with the Soulless Kings, a contract was presented to me. It took several hours to go over the fine print, but basically, I'll be paid an unimaginable sum of money to be Squirrel's lawyer. Along with my 'salary', housing expenses will be covered, provided I allow the club to handle the security of the place and that it has an office space for Squirrel to set up his computer system so he can work behind the scenes.

I was also provided a credit card to utilize for all case expenses, including how I want to handle Alan Forney's fee and lodging expenses. Dude could tell me he wants to live on a private island and there'd still be money left over.

I didn't question where the money came from. The less I know, the better. But I did question the last part of the contract, the part where it said that I agreed to pay back the club seventy-five percent of my salary if I lose the case.

I'd be lying if I didn't admit that I hesitated a bit before signing on the dotted line. But in the end, I couldn't walk away. I know Squirrel is innocent, and I will do whatever it takes to make the justice system see that.

"I think you should at least check it out," Squirrel says, pulling me from my musings.

"For once, I agree with you." I look at Mr. Bunyon. "Do you have time to show us the place now?"

The realtor glances at his watch and then frowns. "I actually have to meet with another client, but I'll text you the code for the lockbox and you can go have a look. All I ask is that you ensure the property is locked up tight when you leave."

"Perfect." I type the code he provides into the notes app

on my phone and reach out to shake his hand. "Thanks again for showing us a few places on such short notice. I'll give you a call after we look at the house."

"You're welcome. And I look forward to hearing from you."

Mr. Bunyon walks out of the penthouse, and we follow him to the elevator. As we reach the first floor, my cell phone rings, and I glance at it to see who's calling.

"Shit," I mutter before ignoring the call and shoving my cell in my pocket.

Squirrel tenses beside me. We both nod at the doorman as we exit the building, but as soon as we're on the sidewalk, Squirrel grabs my arm to stop me.

"Who called?"

I glance at where he's touching me and shake my arm free. "Don't do that again."

Squirrel shoves his hands in his pocket and rocks back on his feet. "Who called?"

Wanting nothing more than to tell him it was no one important and knowing I can't because it likely has to do with his case, I take a deep breath. "It was the prosecutor's office."

"Why didn't you answer?"

"Because I didn't think it was the appropriate time and place to get into it with him." I tilt my head. "Or would you rather I air your dirty laundry and let everyone know you're out on bond for the murder of a child?"

Squirrel's demeanor changes in an instant. He whirls around and slams a fist into the brick wall of the building we just exited. When he pulls his hand back, his knuckles are bleeding, sending crimson droplets to the ground.

"Feel better?"

"Little bit, actually."

*Squirrel*

"Good. Now are you done being a caveman? Because I'd really like to go see that house so I can move on to other things on my to do list."

He swings his arm out in front of him. "Lead the way."

We walk to the end of the street, where my car is parked, in silence. Squirrel dangles his hand like nothing happened, and when I look over my shoulder, I see blood dotting the otherwise clean sidewalk.

I slide into the driver's side and reach into the center console to grab some napkins.

"Here." I thrust them at him. "I'd appreciate it if you could keep the blood in my car to a minimum. I'd like to get something for it when I trade it in."

Squirrel throws his head back and laughs, and I narrow my eyes at him.

"What's so funny?"

"The fact that you think any dealership is going to give you anything for this clunker."

"Of course they will. I've taken excellent care of it. They'd be lucky to have it on their lot."

"Keep telling yourself that."

I huff out a breath and put the car in drive. When I look into the rearview mirror, there's a dark spot on the road, beneath where I was parked.

*Now what's leaking?*

Maybe Squirrel is right. But I'll be damned if I'm going to tell him that.

# Chapter Twelve

*No, baby. That's not how this is going to work.*

### Squirrel

By the time we reach the house, I'm all kinds of frustrated... with the situation, with myself at losing my cool, at my now swelling hand. Oh, and let's not forget sexually. I haven't been this sexually frustrated since I was in high school.

"Are you just going to sit here?"

I turn to face Lexi, who's got the driver's door open with one leg out.

"Fuck no."

"Yeah, didn't think my luck had changed that quick."

I open my door and step out, and we walk to the front door together. She tries to stay ahead of me, but her short legs are no match for my own.

*I'd bet they'd be a perfect match in bed.*

"Why don't you like me?" I blurt out after she gets the door open, and we step inside.

## Squirrel

Lexi stops to turn and look at me. "What?"

"You heard me. Why the hell don't you like me?"

"You can't be serious," she accuses.

"Why?"

She rubs her forehead with one hand while she rests the other on her hip. "Okay, you are serious."

"Damn right I am."

"Well, for starters, you treat me like I'm property that you own and have complete control of. You weren't like that when you were locked up, and I can't quite figure out what's changed. Then there's the fact that you have zero consideration for what I want, what I need. You're arrogant, demanding, insufferable, and, and..."

"And what?"

"A pain in my ass!" Lexi throws her hands up in the air.

"You sure about that? Because what you were doing in the shower this morning says otherwise."

Her eyes widen comically, and the rush of blood to her cheeks tells me she's flustered. "How do you know about that?"

"Well, for starters," I mock her. "You just told me."

All of her bravado leaves on a woosh. "You're an asshole, you know that? I have half a mind to tell you to fuck off and find another attorney."

I take a step toward her. When she doesn't back away, I take another, and then another, until I'm within inches of her body. "We both know you won't do that."

"What makes you think that?"

I can't help but breathe in her scent. I've gotten whiffs of vanilla and honey all day, and to be this close, to inhale her completely, is almost more than I can bear. Almost.

"Because you know I'd go down for a horrific crime that I didn't commit." I reach out and cup her cheek. When she leans into me, it's all I can do not to jump her right here and now. "Because you can't help but do the right thing. And because..." I gently rub my thumb across her skin. "... I think you actually do like me. It scares the shit out of you, but the feeling is still there."

"You don't know what you're talking about," she says breathily.

An idea takes hold. "I'll make you a deal."

She lifts her blue eyes to mine. "I'm listening."

"Kiss me." Before she can protest, I continue. "If you feel nothing, I'll move forward in a professional manner. I'll even go as far as to have one of my brothers handle your security. The only time you'll see me is if it's related to the case."

"And if I do feel something?"

Ah, there it is. She's admitting that there's something here, something that goes beyond attorney-client relationship. And that admittance is all I need. But it's not all I'm going to take. I want that kiss. I need it like I need my next breath.

"If you do, we keep going forward as we are." I shrug. "But with less arguing and fighting me at every turn. You signed the contract, so you knew what was coming."

"I signed a contract for a job, not a relationship."

"Who said anything about a relationship? It's one kiss, Lexi."

"This is ridiculous."

I arch a brow. "How so? It's not like I'm asking you to marry me. Hell, I'm not asking for more than any man on a first date would ask for."

Lexi pushes away from me, and I shiver with the loss of heat.

"But this isn't a date. We're not dating. We've only

known each other for a few days, and it hasn't exactly been under normal circumstances."

"Answer me one question," I say, unwilling to let this go. Now that I've got that kiss in my head, I won't stop until I get it.

"What?"

"Do you know all your first dates as much as you know me? Shit, you know everything about me. Probably too much if we're being honest."

Lexi runs a shaky hand through her dark hair and sighs. "I guess you're right about that."

"So, what harm will one little kiss do?"

"More than you could possibly imagine," she says under her breath.

I pretend I don't hear her words. With as quietly as she said them, that's no doubt what she was going for. But I did hear them.

Lexi takes a deep breath and gives a curt nod. She steps back toward me and looks me square in the eyes. "Fine. Kiss me."

She's standing before me looking like she's about to be executed, not kissed, and that just won't do. I tuck a strand of hair behind her ear, letting my fingers caress her flesh as I do.

I lean in close and whisper, "No, baby. That's not how this is going to work."

Lifting her into my arms, I'm shocked when her legs go around my waist without hesitation. She wants this more than she's willing to admit. Fortunately, her body can't hide her secrets.

I carry her to the kitchen area just beyond the living room. The space is open, and because there's no furniture, I don't have to worry about bumping into anything. As I'm carrying her, we lock eyes. Hers are pools of desire, and I know mine must match.

When we reach the large island, I use one hand to swipe all the spec sheets to the floor before setting her down and stepping between her legs.

I cup both sides of her head, and when I lean forward, her eyes slide closed.

"Look at me," I command.

Lexi's eyes fly open, and she shifts them everywhere but my face.

"Trust me, Lexi."

Her lashes flutter, but she settles her gaze on me.

"Good girl," I coo.

Not wanting to give her any more time to second guess this, I press my lips to hers. Softly at first, but then her tongue darts into my mouth, and I'm lost.

I move my hands to her waist and yank her to the edge of the counter, pressing my ever-growing cock against her center. At the contact, she moans, and the vibrations from that go straight to my dick.

Our tongues clash, doing battle in the most primitive way. I nip at her bottom lip before sucking it into my mouth, intent on making it swell and marking her as mine.

I lose all track of time and space. That is, until my spine starts to tingle. I slow things down, not wanting to embarrass myself, and pull away.

Lexi's wearing a lazy smile, and her lip looks exactly as I intended. Her eyes flutter open, but I can't recall them ever closing.

"Lexi?"

"Hmm?"

"There's so much more where that came from."

*Squirrel*

I lift her off the counter and set her on her feet. She sways, but I steady her.

"Are you always so confident?" she asks.

"When it comes to women and reading them, yes."

"And what are you reading from me?"

"That you liked that more than you'll ever admit. That it scares the shit out of you, but you're not a quitter. You'll stick around, and we'll explore whatever this is. And we'll probably still argue because you're also not the doormat type."

"Would you prefer I was?"

"Not in a million years… Balls."

# Chapter Thirteen

*This is worse somehow.*

**Lexi**

*Two days later...*

"Are you sure you want to do this?"

"You haven't really given me much choice, have you?" I counter.

Squirrel and I sit across from Gregory Firth in the prosecutor's office conference room. When I called him back the other day, he requested a meeting with us both, saying he wanted to review the plea deals with my client himself as he wanted to ensure all information was provided.

*Like I wouldn't do it myself. Asshole.*

"There's always a choice, Lexi. That's something you—"

"Miss Cantor," Squirrel's deep baritone voice interrupts.

Gregory bristles. "Excuse me?"

"Her name is Miss Cantor, or Attorney Cantor. I don't

## Squirrel

believe she's invited you to call her Lexi as that's reserved for friends."

I rest my hand on Squirrel's arm. "It's okay."

"No, it's not. It's disrespectful."

The prosecutor dismisses Squirrel with a wave of his hand. "Whatever. Fine, Miss Cantor."

"Thank you."

Gregory's eyes widen at the display of manners from Squirrel, as if shocked that something so normal could come from someone, in his mind, so vile.

Even Squirrel catches the shock. "What? Not exactly the barn-raised cretin you were expecting?"

Gregory ignores the taunt and shifts his full attention to me. "As I was saying, this is career suicide. You know what you're up against."

I glance at Squirrel out of the corner of my eye and catch his smirk.

*Yeah, I know what I'm up against. And so does he.*

"Please, if you're going to present the plea deals, then do that." I politely smile. "But if you're only going to give me career advice, this meeting is over."

For the next thirty minutes, Squirrel and I sit in silence, listening to Gregory's inflated ego review the details of the deals. The entire time, there's a certainty in his voice that grates on my nerves. It doesn't seem to matter to him how many times he's told no, he still has to push.

When he's done, he leans back casually in his chair. "Now, Mr. Kramer, these are terrific deals, and I'd advise—"

"Mr. Firth, I will remind you that Mr. Kramer is my client, therefore the only advice that's warranted is mine." I stare him in the eyes as I speak and remind myself that I can't stoop to his level, no matter how hard I want to bitch slap him. "It is highly inappropriate for you to overstep the way you have." I stand from my chair, and Squirrel follows suit. "We're done here."

I lead Squirrel out of the room, and when we reach the elevator, I can still hear the prosecutor blustering about something. I shocked him. Good. There's a lot more where that came from.

When we step out onto the sidewalk in front of the building, I breathe in the fresh air. Anytime I'm in a room with Gregory Firth, I feel robbed of all that's good in the world, all that's clean and pure. And when I leave, I feel the overpowering need to shower because the man makes my skin crawl.

I lift my eyes to Squirrel, who's standing next to me while we wait for the all clear for the crosswalk.

"Think all my stuff is moved?"

A group of Soulless Kings' brothers were moving my stuff from the apartment to the new rental while we were in our meeting. I spent yesterday packing, although admittedly there wasn't a lot. It shouldn't take them long at all.

"Maybe. But I'd say it's more likely that they're fucking off. Bug will certainly be a distraction for them."

I can't help but laugh picturing Bug's antics and a bunch of bikers running around playing with him. Something tells me that they're all as big a lug as he is.

"What's next on the agenda?" Squirrel asks. "You ready to go home or do you have more to do in town?"

"I think I want to go home," I say, feeling a headache coming on and desperately wanting that shower. "I've got more to do, but it can wait for now."

"Okay, if you're sure?"

"I'm sure."

## Squirrel

The drive to the rental house is quiet. Squirrel is behind the wheel, insisting that he drive, and I stare out the window watching as we move beyond the buildings toward wide open spaces. When we reach the house, there is one moving truck, several Harley's, and a delivery truck with a man stepping out of the driver's side.

"I wonder what that is?" Squirrel muses aloud. "Did you order anything?"

I shake my head.

"Stay here, let me check it out."

He exits the car, and at the same time, Fender and Sling step out onto the porch. The three of them converge on the delivery guy until he backs himself up against his truck. Needing to know what's going on, I get out of my car and walk to stand next to them in time to hear the bikers' questioning the poor guy.

"Who sent you?"

"What do ya have in there?"

Question after question until the man holds his hands up.

"Please, I have a delivery for a..." He glances down at the documentation in his hand and then returns his attention to them. "... Squirrel?" He shakes his head. "No, no, that can't be right."

"I'm Squirrel."

The driver eyes him up and down, and I can see his throat bob when he swallows.

"Oh, um... here."

He walks away from them toward the back of the truck and opens the door. When Squirrel looks in, he whistles.

"Hot damn, are you a sight for sore eyes."

Squirrel walks up the ramp once the driver has it

secured, and the next thing I hear is a loud roar. He reappears on the back of a Harley, and the wide grin on his face is priceless.

"Check it out, Lexi." He guides the bike toward me. "Steel perfection."

The driver requests a signature, and Squirrel obliges. Once the back of the truck is closed and the driver opens his door, Squirrel stops him.

"Sorry about the welcoming committee buddy." He claps him on the shoulder. "You can never be too careful."

"Right. No problem." The driver reaches into the cab of his truck, and when he turns back to face Squirrel, he thrusts an envelope at him. "Here, this came with it. Have a nice day."

The delivery man makes quick work of backing out of the driveway and disappearing down the road. Fender and Sling move closer to Squirrel, looking over his shoulder to see what's in the envelope. I stay back, not knowing if I have any right to see it.

Squirrel reads the note and then shows it to his brothers. All three of them throw their heads back on a laugh, and that's when I can no longer resist the temptation.

"Can I see it?"

Squirrel turns the piece of paper toward me, and when I read the words, I roll my eyes.

*Take the girl for a ride. No female can resist the buzz of a Harley between their legs.*
  *-Charlie & the ladies*

"Who's Charlie?" I ask and immediately wish I could call the words back.

Fender throws his arm around my shoulder. "Charlie is

*Squirrel*

my wife, so shove that little green monster off your shoulder. And the rest of the ladies are spoken for too. I'm sure Squirrel would rather have his dick cut off than mess with any of them."

I shove my glasses up my nose, trying to mask my discomfort and embarrassment at having asked the question. It's none of my business who Squirrel dates, even if that kiss felt like it should be.

"Right."

Squirrel clears his throat. "You know I'm right here, right?" he asks, still on his bike.

Fender guides me toward the front door, leaving Squirrel behind. He chuckles before responding. "Of course we do."

When I enter my new house, Bug comes running toward me, sliding on the hardwood floor and crashing into my legs. I bend down to scratch his ears and let him rain kisses on me.

"I'd say you approve, huh buddy?"

Bug barks before racing back in the direction he came from. My living room is full of boxes, but none of my furniture is here. Oh, there's furniture, just not mine.

"Before you say anything, consider it a housewarming gift," Sling says as he walks toward me, no doubt seeing my shocked expression. "Squirrel said you'd want something sophisticated and comfortable. Steph went shopping yesterday with a few of the other ol' ladies, and this..." He indicates the brand-new sleek couch, chairs, and coffee table. "... is what they came up with."

I sit down on the couch, running my hands over the blue velvet couch, luxuriating in the soft fabric. "It's perfect."

I jump up and launch myself at Sling, wrapping my arms around his neck. "Thank you so much."

"I think he gets the message."

Sling drops me to my feet, and I whirl around to see Squirrel standing in the doorway with his arms crossed over his chest, his own feet spread apart. He looks so upset that guilt washes over me.

I close the distance between us and wrap my arms around his waist. He's hesitant at first, but I don't know whether it's because we're surrounded by his friends or because he doesn't want this. After a few seconds, his arms engulf me in a hug.

"Thank you," I say into his chest.

He leans down to whisper, "You're welcome."

When I disengage from him, I face the others. "I can't thank you all enough for helping me get moved in. It means a lot that total strangers would do this for me."

"We're not strangers, Balls," Joker says. "And something tells me we're all about to get to know each other a lot better."

Nerves settle into the pit of my stomach, but I don't know why. These guys don't scare me anymore, so that's not it. Maybe it's the prospect of getting to know them, really know them, that scares me. As someone who is proud to follow the letter of the law, I know it's going to be hard to see certain things.

I choose to ignore Joker's comment and focus on Sling. "I'd like to thank Steph and the others, as well. Would it be okay if I stopped by the clubhouse later?"

"Actually, we insist that you do. We've got a party tonight, and you're the guest of honor."

My hand flies to my chest. I've never been the guest of honor for anything.

## *Squirrel*

"I'll be there."

"Great." Sling moves toward the door, and the others follow. Well, all except Squirrel. "See you later then."

Once the rumble of Harleys diminishes, I return to the couch, wanting to feel the decadence again. Squirrel sits next to me and slings his arm over the back.

"I really appreciate the furniture," I say.

"Don't mention it."

Before I can respond, the couch vibrates. Squirrel pulls a cell phone out of his pocket, and I narrow my eyes at him.

"You're not supposed to have a cell phone. That was a condition of your bond. No phones, computers, access to internet."

"And yet you signed a contract agreeing to having an office for me in your home," he counters.

I huff out a breath, knowing he's right. I guess I need to really think about where and how I can draw the line while still adhering to the terms I agreed to.

"Besides, it's untraceable, a burner."

"Oh and that makes it so much better," I mumble.

Squirrel flips open the phone—yes, it's one of those old school ones—and his body goes rigid.

"What is it?" I ask.

"Nobody has this number but the club."

"I should have it too, by the way. But what does that have to do with anything?"

"It's a text from an unknown number."

"And..." I prompt.

"And shit just got real."

He turns the screen so I can see it, and my blood runs cold. He's wrong, shit was already real. I mean, hello, murder charge.

But this?

This is worse somehow.

**You should have taken the plea deals. Instead you brought the girl into it. Now her life is in your hands.**

# Chapter Fourteen

*The Nightmare Room is calling my name, begging me to use it.*

**Squirrel**

"Would everyone shut the fuck up?"

I slam my fists on the table, and the room gradually goes silent. As soon as I got that text, I sent out an alert to my brothers, and two hours later? Well, here we are.

"Could've handled that, Squirrel," Fender says dryly.

"No offense, Prez, but you weren't."

"Watch it," Sling seethes. "Your prez may put up with that kinda shit, but I don't."

"Neither do I," Fender agrees. "Squirrel, it happens again, and you're done. I suggest you don't let it happen."

"I make no promises." I thrust a hand through my hair. "This is frustrating as hell. Isn't it bad enough that they're trying to ruin my life? Why'd they have to bring Lexi into it?"

"In case you haven't noticed," Joker says. "She's in it, brother. All the way up to the nerdy glasses that refuse to stay on her nose."

"It's bullshit," I bark. "She's done nothing wrong."

"She's going up against what I can only assume are pretty powerful people. Add to that that she's potentially ruining someone's big payday? She's going to have issues. All of which are dangerous."

"Listen," Fender says, his tone inviting no arguments. "Before we can figure out how to stop the danger to Lexi, we have to fight Squirrel's battle. They're linked. Fix one problem, fix them all."

"Agreed," Sling says.

"And how do we do that?" I ask. "Because so far, all we know is that I'm being set up for a murder charge and that there are plenty of higher ups who can be bought."

"We start at the beginning," Flash says, having been quiet up until now. "Squirrel, we are here because we trust you. We know who you are, and it's not a child killer. But you've gotta tell us why it's so easy for the cops and prosecutors to pin it on you."

Until this moment, it hadn't occurred to me that my brothers, my family, have blindly supported me, no questions asked. It's how it is with us. We have each other's backs no matter what. But for them to have mine, even with something this fucking huge... it means a lot.

"I've tried to come up with a reason they think they can prove I did it beyond a reasonable doubt, and there's nothing. Lexi's looked through all the reports, and there's no DNA, no fingerprints, no murder weapon... nothing."

"But you were at that motel that night?" Fender asks for clarification.

I nod. "I was on my way home from visiting the New

## Squirrel

Jersey chapter. It's a long ass drive, and I stopped three times. Once, here in Michigan, and again in Iowa and Wyoming. I don't remember much about the night I was here." I implore them with my eyes. "You know me, guys. I grabbed shit from the vending machines and stayed in my room."

"And you didn't leave at all? It was mentioned in one of the reports that they have you on camera close to the victim's room."

"I saw that too. The only thing I can think of is when I went to grab some ice. Based on the layout of the motel that the cops obtained, there's a machine right around the corner from the room."

"Have you seen the video footage they claim to have?" Joker asks.

I shake my head. "I don't even know if it's been provided to the defense. I'll ask Lexi though. If she hasn't gotten it yet, she will."

"Good. Once you have it, load it up into your fancy programs and figure out if that shit was doctored."

"Oh, you bet your ass I'm gonna go over it with a fine-toothed comb."

"What about the girl? Do you remember seeing her at all?"

"No. There were several prostitutes hanging around the parking lot when I got there, but I wasn't in the mood. Besides, they all looked way too young." I shrug. "But I guess one of them could have been her. I saw the photographs in evidence, and she was so beat up I didn't recognize her as being one of them though."

Flashes of the girl race through my mind, one by one. When I was interrogated, pictures were slapped in front of me, no doubt to gauge my reaction, and those are the images

I see now. Fortunately, I have a strong stomach because otherwise, I'd have puked all over the state's precious evidence. Maria Sampson suffered, and I wouldn't wish that kind of pain on anyone, especially a child.

*There are some you'd wish it on. Hell, there are some you've inflicted it on.*

But never a child.

"Jesus, I can only imagine what she looked like," Flash grumbles.

"Well, you won't have to imagine for long. We're all going to have to sit down and sift through all the evidence, piece by piece, if we want to get ahead of this," Fender reminds him.

"Fun times."

"Nothing about this is fun," I snap, annoyed with Flash for downplaying the situation.

"You're right," he agrees. "It's not. Sorry."

"Before we get too far down the rabbit hole, can I add my two cents?" Sling asks.

"Absolutely, brother," Fender says. "We always welcome another chapter's input."

Sling sits in the empty chair next to mine and leans forward to rest his forearms on the table.

"I think you're missing the bigger picture here."

"How so?" Greaser asks.

"The first thing you need to do is get Squirrel out from under this murder charge and then you all need to get gone back to Oregon."

"If we're oversta—"

Sling waves a hand dismissively. "No, no, nothing like that. You know you're all welcome here any fucking time you want. But this isn't about Squirrel's guilt or innocence. Everyone knows he's innocent, even the prosecutor. So what is it that the more powerful people are being blackmailed to do? It has to be something with the club, right? Since the FBI offered a plea deal for info on the Soulless Kings."

Sling pauses and looks around the room. When he's not met with any argument or question, he continues.

"Lexi has that tape that proves the prosecutor is taking a bribe and implicates people in the FBI. Use it."

"If we use it, we can't make them suffer," I seethe, wanting to watch dominoes fall one at a time. "I need them to suffer."

"You can still make them suffer," Sling counters. "It'll just look different." He focuses his attention on me. "Look, I get it. You want to rip apart the people trying to, well, rip you apart. But Gregory Firth is a small fish. Quite frankly, so are the individuals in the FBI who are paying him. If you want revenge that tastes as sweet as pussy, you find the top dog and treat him to a staycation, Soulless Kings' style.

"What he's saying makes sense." Flash leans forward. "It would be the fastest way to a conclusion."

Rage boils in my blood until it bubbles to the surface. I flatten my palms on the table and stand.

"I don't want fast. I want slow and excruciating."

The idea of anyone involved getting away with this triggers the undeniable need to inflict as much pain and devastation as I can. The Nightmare Room is calling my name, begging me to use it.

"What about Lexi?" Greaser asks quietly. "Because there's a chance that she'll suffer too."

And just like that, my pent-up rage quiets inside of me. The Nightmare Room fades away, and all I'm left with is the intense need to protect her. Fuck myself, she's more important.

*Why?*

Before this—shit, as little as a week ago—I was a confirmed bachelor. I was content to have meaningless sex with nameless women, as long as they satisfied that night's itch.

And then I was handcuffed to a table when a pie-in-the-sky, glasses wearing, sexy attorney walked in the room... late.

I'm not an emotional man by any stretch of the imagination. I'm not one to wax poetic or some such bullshit. Nor am I the type who wants to be all in touch with my feelings. But Lexi tugs at all those things and makes me want to do better, be better.

It makes no fucking sense. But who am I to question it?

"We run it by her and get her input," I concede. "I don't want her hurt, but I'm not willing to give up on revenge either."

"That's fair," Fender agrees. "For now, why don't we discuss plans so we're prepared to move forward with the trial, or use the tape so we can put all of our resources into finding the one pulling the strings in this hellish puppet show?"

"I have one request before we discuss plans."

"And what's that?"

"If Lexi agrees on using the tape, that will effectively end her association with us. Do we have it in the budget to at least let her keep the original two hundred and fifty grand we gave her?" I keep my attention focused on Fender and Flash, as they're going to be the two key people in this answer. "I don't want her moving back to that shithole she called home."

"If Fender's okay with it, we can swing it financially," Flash says.

## Squirrel

I lock eyes with Fender. "Well, Prez?"

Fender looks at Joker and Greaser and each gives an almost imperceptible nod. He returns his attention to me.

"I'll do you one better than that. If that's what she wants, yes, I'll agree to it. But I'll also keep the offer on the table for her to come to Oregon to work as the club's attorney. Forney is becoming a joke, and I was planning on doing away with him when this was all over. Method still to be determined." His lips tilt into a sinister grin at that. "Besides, as it stands, trial or no trial, she's in this and she's going to be in danger until we ferret these fuckers out. She'll be safer with us anyway."

"Then let's get this shit figured out."

# Chapter Fifteen

*Just how crazy are those Oregon fuckers?*

**Lexi**

"How long you been sittin' here, hun?"

I lift my eyes from my phone to the woman behind the bar and stare at her like she has two heads. I've been in the clubhouse several times, but this is the first where I've been left alone. When we arrived, Squirrel led me to the bar and told me he'd be back in a while. That was two hours ago.

I shrug. "A while."

The woman is dressed in a black leather lace up top that leaves nothing to the imagination, and her shorts rest low on her hips. There's a shiny belly-button ring that sparkles in between. Her long blonde hair is curled, and there's pink streaks running generously through the strands. She is gorgeous, and suddenly I feel very self-conscious.

## Squirrel

"Who are you here with?" she asks, almost seemingly to fill the silence.

"Squirrel. He's meeting with the others." My glasses slip, so I push them up, which makes me feel even more inferior. "I'm Squirrel's attorney, Lexi Cantor."

"You're Balls?" She looks at me with disbelief. "Sorry, it's just that you're not at all what I was expecting." She sticks her hand out. "I'm Courtney, Sling's sister-in-law and bartender extraordinaire."

I shake her hand. "Nice to meet you."

"You too. Let me get you something to drink."

Before I can tell her what I want, or even *if* I want anything, she moves to the other end of the bar and reaches under it. When she returns, she sets a glass of red wine down and slides it toward me.

"You look like a wine person to me."

I'm not sure if that was meant as a compliment or not, but I let it go. She's right and it doesn't matter why. I take a sip of the crimson liquid and let it coat my tongue. It's good. Really good.

"Like it?" Courtney asks.

"Very much." I lift the glass to gaze into its liquid contents. "What is it?"

Courtney grins. "I'm not sure I should tell you."

"Listen, I drink wine from a box because it's all I can afford." I smirk. "You can tell me."

She throws her head back and laughs but quickly pulls herself together. "Ya know what, Balls? You're my kind of people."

I tilt my head, waiting for her to go on.

She nods toward the glass in my hand. "That there is Black Box Cabernet Sauvignon... a.k.a boxed wine." Courtney winks. "The only thing Sling stocks the bar with is local beers, but Steph likes wine. He lets her have this, insisting that it's just low class enough that it doesn't offend his alcoholic sensibilities."

I set the now empty glass down and consider it. "Makes sense, I suppose. In a weird sort of way."

"Everything they do makes sense... in a weird sort of way." Courtney's attention is drawn to the door, and she smiles and waves. "Here comes trouble."

Steph strides across the room and then sits on the stool next to mine. She glares at Courtney and then shifts her disdain to me. I've only met her once and can't help but wonder if I did something to piss her off.

"Talking shit about me again, Court?"

Courtney feigns shock and places her hand on her chest. "Me? Never."

"Whatever," Steph twists to face me. "So, all moved in?"

"Thanks to Sling and the others, yes. Still have to unpack though. We got sidetracked by a text Squirrel received."

"Yeah, that's what Sling said." She pats me on the back. "Don't worry. They'll get it all sorted out and make sure nothing happens to you."

"I'm not worried," I lie.

I'm very worried. I still barely know these people, and not only have I trusted them with my career, but now I may have to trust them with my life. Shit, I'm a walking poster child for bad decisions lately.

"Of course you are," Steph counters. "But you shouldn't be. I can only speak personally for the Michigan chapter, but they've handled some pretty fucked up shit and come out on top. As for the mother chapter of Soulless Kings... I've heard the stories. If ever there's a group of men that can handle whatever is thrown their way, it's them." She leans in close and adds, "Don't tell Sling I said that, or I just might end up in the Nightmare Room. He's got an ego on him."

There's humor in her voice so I know she's teasing, but my brain snags on two words.

"Nightmare Room?"

Steph throws her arm around my shoulder and pulls me close. "If you've got half as big a set as the guys say you do, you'll love it."

I don't know about that. Anything with the word 'nightmare' attached sounds terrifying. These people seem to think that because I can stand up to a prosecutor and do what I deem the right thing, it means I can take on the world. Who knows? Maybe they're right. I've never been put in the position to really see what I can handle.

And if they're wrong?

Well, I guess I'll find out.

"So, Balls, you and Squirrel sticking around the rest of the day until the party?" Courtney asks after filling my wine glass, pulling me from my musings.

"I doubt it. I've got things to do today." I glance down at my outfit. "And I suppose I'll need to change."

Courtney and Steph exchange a look and grin.

"Are you thinking what I'm thinking?" Steph asks Courtney.

Courtney looks over my shoulder. "Yo, Clown!" she hollers. I glance behind me and see a man pop up from the couch. *How did I not see him earlier?* "Hold down the fort. Steph and I are leaving."

When Clown stands, Steph shakes her head. "And put some fucking pants on."

Clown runs a hand through his already disheveled hair and scratches his chest. His junk is standing loud and proud, and I avert my eyes.

"Jesus, can't a guy enjoy a wet dream without being interrupted by a few harpies?" he grumbles as he makes his way toward a hallway.

"You love us," Steph calls out to him.

"Yeah, yeah."

"Don't mind him," Courtney tells me. "He's a grump when he first wakes up."

"So am I." I look back at the couch he was laying on. "Remind me never to sit on that thing."

Both women laugh. It's a few minutes before Clown reappears and stands behind the bar with Courtney.

"The others are in a meeting. Tell 'em we'll be back in time for the party," Steph instructs him.

He glances at me and then back to Steph. "She going too?"

"She is right here," I snap, annoyed at once again being talked about like I'm not in the room. "And yes." I nod making the quick decision. "I'm going."

"Just tell them, okay?"

"Fine," Clown agrees. "But it'll be your heads if they don't like it."

"Don't you worry about us. I can handle Sling," Steph says with a sly grin on her face.

"It's not Sling I'm worried about, Steph. It's those Oregon fuckers. They're crazy."

With those final words, Courtney and Steph seem to descend on me and whisk me away, and I'm left to wonder one thing:

Just how crazy are those Oregon fuckers?

# Chapter Sixteen

*She doesn't look as happy to see me as my dick is to see her.*

**Squirrel**

"Feel any better about shit, bro?"

Flash slaps me on the back as we exit the meeting room. We figured out a plan and looped in the rest of the voting members in Oregon via conference call. Fender can make decisions, but always prefers to vote when necessary.

"A little." I scrub my hands over my face. "I'll feel even better when I've got more sophisticated equipment hooked up back at Lexi's place and can do my own digging into information."

"And that can wait until tomorrow. For now, we've got a party to get ready for."

We walk down the hall to the main room of the clubhouse. "Lexi has some things to do, so I think I'll skip out on party prep and go with her."

The crowd is growing, and the party isn't for another

few hours. Based on the sea of cuts, only club members are present, but if it's anything like back home, that'll change. I look around for Lexi and don't see her, so I go up to the bar.

"Yo." I glance at the man's cut. "Clown. Any idea where Lexi is?"

"Who?"

"Dark haired chick, about this tall." I hold my hand up to my chest to indicate her height.

"Doesn't really narrow it down."

I grunt out my frustration. "She was wearing jeans and a tee and wears glasses that like to slip down her nose. Real cute."

Clown's face lights up and then falls. "Oh, yeah. She left with Steph and Courtney."

I grip the edge of the bar and growl, "When?"

He shrugs. "A while ago."

I shove myself away from the ledge and stomp toward the door. Anger burns inside of me. What the hell was she thinking? She saw that text, she knows what kind of danger she's in.

*Does she? You didn't exactly explain things to her.*

I remind myself that Lexi isn't from this world. She's obviously aware that there is evil out there, that bad people exist. But has she ever really experienced the darker side that sits just beneath the surface, scratching its way through until it sucks all the good down into the pits of Hell?

"Squirrel, what's going on?" Greaser asks, falling into step beside me. "You look like you're about to do something stupid."

I whirl on him. "Lexi's gone."

"What do you mean, gone?"

"She went with Steph and Courtney." I cross my arms

over my chest. "Just left and didn't tell anyone where she was going."

Fender and Sling join us, and they must have caught what I said because Sling says, "You mean, she didn't tell *you* where she was going."

"Exactly." When the three of them get smirks on their faces, I throw my hands up in the air. "What?" I bark.

"If I know my ol' lady, they're probably shopping." Sling slips his cell phone out of his pocket. "I'll call and make sure."

He steps away for a few minutes, leaving me to seethe and Fender and Greaser to stare at me with teasing grins.

"Jesus, take a picture, it'll last longer."

"Nah, brother." Fender punches me on the shoulder. "We don't need a picture. We're gonna be seeing you like this for quite a while."

"What's that supposed to mean?"

"It means," Greaser starts. "Buckle up buttercup because you're about to take the ride of your life."

Before I can process what they're saying, Sling returns.

"I was right. They took Lexi to get something to wear tonight. They're at a shop downtown."

I turn around and walk through the door, out into the fresh air. The three of them follow.

"Where are you going?"

I stride toward my Harley. "To bring Lexi back," I say without slowing.

"Oh, I'm so in for this," Greaser says, and I hear his footsteps behind me.

"G, let him go," Fender orders. "You and I both know how this is going to end for him. Let him figure it out."

"But Prez," Greaser begins.

It's on the tip of my tongue to throw shade at them both

for acting like a couple of chicks, but I'm too focused on getting to Lexi and giving her a piece of my mind.

I fire up my bike and tear out of the circular drive of the clubhouse. No one follows.

Once I reach town, I ride up and down each street, looking for her car. When I don't see it, a fresh wave of panic hits me. I find a parking space and leave my Harley to go looking on foot.

As I'm walking in and out of shops, the stares full of judgment and fear aren't lost on me. I saw the posters, the ones with my mug shot and Maria Sampson's face plastered on them, the ones that say 'Justice for Maria'. Of course they're all afraid of me. They think I'm a murderer.

I'm used to these looks, the assumptions and judgment, but it's always been based on my appearance, even though I'm the least scary of the Soulless Kings'. Fuck, I'm a tech whiz. I'm as nerdy as a biker gets without looking like a nerd.

After a half hour, I come to the last shop. I yank open the door, and all eyes turn to me. Lexi better be in here or so help—

"Squirrel?"

I turn toward the dressing room area and see Courtney and Steph there, each with their arms loaded down with clothes.

"What are you doing here?" Steph asks. "I told Sling we were fine."

"Where is she?"

I slide my hands in my pockets to hide the fact that they're balled into fists. I would never hurt any of them, but I've worked myself up to deliver a good verbal lashing.

The curtain to the dressing room slides open and Lexi steps out, arms crossed over her chest and every last bit of air leaves the room. My lungs seize and my jaw drops. Unfortunately, she doesn't look as happy to see me as my dick is to see her.

My gaze travels from her toes to her head, and I don't bother to hide my appreciation for what I see.

On Lexi's feet are three-inch red spiked heels. Her legs are covered in dark wash jeans with rips up the length of them so a hint of inner thigh peeks out. And her chest? Holy fuck, her chest. Lexi's cleavage spills over a tight red tee that has the deepest V at the neck I've ever seen.

The flash of skin between the hem of her shirt and jeans taunts me, begs me to trace my fingertips around her waist. I flex my hands in my pockets because if I make the slightest move to follow through with my desires, I'll fuck her right here in front of everyone.

"I believe she asked you a question."

I lift my eyes from Lexi's boobs to her face and try to swallow past the cotton in my mouth. "Huh?"

"What the hell are you doing here?"

"I, uh..." *C'mon, man, get your shit together.* "Your car isn't outside."

*Smooth.*

"Yes, it is," Lexi insists.

The anger in her eyes hasn't diminished at all, despite my obvious discomfort.

"You should see it, Squirrel," Courtney cuts in. "I wish I could afford a car like that."

My brains scramble a little more. A car like that? Lexi's car is a hunk of junk.

*The money.*

"You got a new car?" I ask, even more distracted away from the reason I'm here.

Lexi lifts a shoulder. "Figured it was time."

"Good." My head bobs like an idiot. "That's good. What'd you get?"

"It's parked out front if you wanna take a look," she responds.

I walk back toward the front of the shop and peer out the glass windows. Parked right on the street is a 1967 Black Chevy Impala. The car is immaculate, shining like she drove it off the showroom floor all those years ago. And I should know. Next to motorcycles and tech shit, classic cars are kind of a passion of mine.

Sensing Lexi before I see her, I glance to my left.

"You like it?" she asks.

"What's not to like?" I ask, never taking my eyes off her. "Where'd you get it?"

Lexi's cheeks darken, and no doubt she caught my double meaning, but she glosses over it. "Saw an ad online and called the guy. Turns out you all were right, money talks."

"And you got all this done since you ditched me back at the clubhouse?"

Her shoulders stiffen, and I want to call the words back. Talking about the car was safe, and I just tugged her back over that line to unsafe.

"I didn't ditch you, Squirrel," she says. "I went shopping."

"Without telling me."

"I wasn't aware that I had to give you a blow by blow of my movements."

I lift my arm, and she flinches, causing me to pause.

"What was that?" I ask cautiously.

Lexi huffs out a breath. "In case you didn't notice, I'm not wearing my glasses. You're a bit blurry."

Damn, I hadn't noticed. I was too focused on her body. I

## Squirrel

take in her eyes, her lashes, her minimal makeup, all unguarded by black rimmed glasses. She's a beautiful woman, and I would think that regardless of her eyewear, but the glasses just do something for me.

"Why aren't you wearing them?"

*Shut up, dude. Quit finding buttons to push.*

"Because, if you must know, I took them off when I changed shirts. They kept falling off anyway, so that was easier. Then," she narrows her eyes. "I heard your voice."

"Oh." I rock back on my heels, determined to turn this situation around. "I like the car."

Her shoulders sag. "Me too."

"I'm still mad that you left without telling me."

Lexi goes rigged again. So much for turning things around.

"Too damn bad. You're not my keeper."

"Maybe not, but you saw that text."

She glances around the store and lowers her voice, as if people will overhear some top-secret details.

"Yes, I saw it. And yes, it scared me. But I'm with them." She hitches a thumb over her shoulder toward Steph and Courtney, who are standing there glaring. "I'm fine."

"Look, I came here ready to read you the riot act. I'm beginning to understand that was a mistake. But mark my words, Lexi, we're going to talk about this later. Things are a lot more dangerous than I think you realize."

"Fine, we'll talk later. For now, you need to leave."

I chuckle. "Yeah, that's not happening. I won't get in your way, but I'm not going anywhere until you do."

"You can't be serious," she huffs out.

"Deadly."

Lexi turns on her heel and struts away from me. I gotta say, watching her leave is almost as satisfying as staring at her standing still. My mouth waters at the images that thought conjures up, and I swallow the extra saliva.

"I'll be outside," I tell the three of them and walk toward the check out. I pull out a wad of cash and drop it on the counter in front of the slack-jawed cashier.

"Anything she wants, she gets." I nod toward the money. "Oh, and make sure that outfit she's wearing is in that bag when she leaves."

The cashier finally gains her composure and grins.

"You got it."

# Chapter Seventeen

*I put up the closed sign on my old life and took a chance on hanging an open sign on a life they thrust me into.*

**Lexi**

Leaning over the sink to look at my reflection in the bathroom mirror, I can't help but wonder what the hell I'm doing. I signed a contract to work for people I barely know, quit my job, moved and bought a new car. I glance down at the bag on the floor. Not to mention purchased clothes I'd never in a million years have contemplated prior to last week.

*Squirrel paid for them.*

That makes it even worse somehow. Oh my God, I'm a bought woman. Bought and paid for by money that was obtained who knows how, and now I'm saddled with a man who plagues my every thought.

*How did I get here?*

That's a damn good question. It's been days, not weeks or months or any other amount of time that would make my choices make sense. Lust, attraction, overachiever mentality. Call it what you want, it doesn't make it any less of a problem.

Maybe my parents were right. Maybe I should have listened and tried to get a cushy job at some big law firm back in New York. Life would sure be easier.

*Would it though?*

"Everything okay in there?"

Squirrel's voice comes through the door, and I swipe at the tears I didn't even realize were flowing.

"Yeah," I say, unable to hide the crack in my voice. "I'll be out in a minute."

I listen for retreating footsteps, but when they don't come, I take a deep breath. "Hey, can you take Bug out for me?" I ask, needing him to walk away.

He sighs, although it's barely audible through the door. "Sure."

The footsteps come, and I breathe a sigh of relief. When we returned to my house so I could change, Squirrel tried to start a conversation and explain why he was so upset. I didn't want to hear it, so I locked myself in the bathroom. I know when I go back out there, he's going to want to talk, and I don't know if I'm ready.

I assure myself that there are no more tears on my cheeks and step out of the bathroom. No time like the present to face the music. It has to happen, whether I'm ready or not.

I grab a bottle of water from the fridge and lean against the island. Staring at the still unpacked boxes, I wait for Squirrel and Bug to come back inside. When they do, Bug does his usual racing around but manages to calm down after I give him a treat.

## *Squirrel*

"You sure you're okay?" Squirrel asks, leaning next to me.

I nod.

"Bullshit." He faces me and then turns me to face him. "Lexi, talk to me."

My barely tethered control snaps.

"I don't know you!" I yell.

"Finally."

"Excuse me?"

"You've got all this bravado inside of you, all of this fire, but you keep it bottled up. Even when you're standing up for yourself, you're holding back." He flattens his hand on my chest. "*This* is why I wanted to hire you outside of the public defender's office. Your heart."

"My heart has nothing to do with this."

"It has everything to do with this," he counters. "Your passion for the law, your need to get things right, is why you're here. Without that, I'd probably still be sitting in a jail cell."

"I doubt that."

"I don't," he says gruffly. "Sure, Soulless Kings have money and connections. But it was your gut that told you to record that meeting with the prosecutor. I'll concede that I may have gotten out on bail, but I would've been right back in that jail cell eventually."

I stand there, stony, silent. Squirrel removes his hand and lets his arm fall to his side.

"Can I ask you something?"

I lift my eyes to his. "Yeah."

"Why did you sign that contract? I know why *I* think you did, but I want to hear why you *actually* did."

That's a loaded question, one even I'm not sure how to

answer. I've thought about it, from the moment I took their money and signed my name, I've played my reasons over and over in my head. Problem is, I have yet to determine if I'm just trying to convince myself I made the best call or if I was right.

"I don't know."

"Sure you do," he counters. "Just give me the first reason that came to mind."

"Because someone had to be one hundred percent on your side," I blurt out.

"Okay. And another reason."

"Because I hate Gregory Firth. I can't stand to see bad people being touted as heroes, always getting away with everything because of their status."

"Okay." He tips my chin with a finger. "There's more to it, though. I can tell."

I pull away from him and move to the couch, where I sit down and pull a pillow into my lap. Squirrel joins me.

*You've jumped, Lexi. When you signed that contract, you took a leap of faith, and you have to see it through.*

"You wouldn't understand." I try one more time to stop this line of questioning.

"Try me."

Bug jumps up and rests his head on my lap. Him being near is what gives me the ability to dive in.

"I've spent my entire life being told what to do, how to do it, when to do it. My parents were strict in their beliefs and raised me in a way that left no room for my own wants and needs. They had a dream for me, and it didn't matter if mine lined up or not." I pull Bug closer, needing more of his comfort. "I was groomed from birth to do whatever it took so I could grow up and be a success so I could take care of them."

## Squirrel

"Isn't that sort of the order of things? We tend to switch roles with our parents as they get older."

"It was more than that. I saw how hard my parents worked. My dad worked long hours as a mechanic to provide for us, and when my mom wasn't working, she was taking care of the entire community. Little time was left over for me, unless it was to tell me I could do better than an A- on a test or to badger me to decide what college to go to. They always wanted more from me."

I pause and glance at Squirrel. He's watching me intently, interest clear in his expression.

"At the time, I thought it was normal. I didn't know any better. And while our dreams for me weren't the same, they were heading down similar tracks, so I shoved it all aside and worked as hard as I could to make sure I made it to law school." I lick my lips and lean my head back against the couch. "Man, they were so proud of me when I graduated law school. I think that was the first time I'd seen them genuinely proud of me. And I soaked it up. But it didn't last. They wanted their daughter to be some rich, high-powered attorney in New York, while all I wanted to do was help people."

"Well, you've managed the rich part," he teases, bumping his shoulder into mine.

I give a watery laugh, realizing since I started talking that I've been crying again. "True." I flap my hand. "Anyway, the job market back home sucked, but then I got the job at the public defender's office. I was ecstatic. They were... disappointed. They felt I wouldn't be able to provide them the lifestyle they wanted for their older years, and they were right. I couldn't. I sent money when I could, but not a lot. We don't talk much anymore, unless they need something. I even called to tell them I quit my job, and they couldn't even muster up any happiness for me because it still didn't equate to more money for them."

"I'm sorry. Parents shouldn't put that kind of burden on their children."

"The thing is, I would've taken care of them. I would have made sure that they had what they needed to live comfortable lives. It just wasn't happening fast enough for them. As much as they hate me, I love them."

"Of course you do," he coos. There's a brief silence before he talks again. "Can I ask what this has to do with why you signed the contract?"

I don't think he really didn't get the point of my story, but I'll spell it out for him anyway.

"I *hate* being told what to do. By anyone. My parents told me to have a more lucrative career. My old boss told me to talk you into a plea deal. Gregory Firth told me to take a bribe. I couldn't keep doing it." I twist on the cushion to face him. "Not one time did any of you tell me what to do. I signed the contract because there wasn't a gun to my head forcing me to do it. It was my decision and my decision alone."

"Makes sense."

"On top of that, the contract offers me opportunities at almost every milestone to back out if I want. Contract or not, no one is holding me to the position."

"And that's what I wanted to talk to you about earlier."

"What do you mean?"

"This is one of those milestones, an opportunity for you to back out, no questions asked."

"And if I'm not ready to back out?"

"Then don't," Squirrel says. "But at least hear me out first, and then make your decision."

I twist to face him, pulling my leg beneath me. Bug

adjusts and takes a minute to complete his circles before he's comfortable again.

"What now?" I finally ask.

Squirrel snaps his fingers like he's forgotten something and then takes his cell phone out of his pocket.

"What are you doing?"

"Texting Fender to tell him we're not going to make it to the party."

"But what about the outfit I bought?" It's such a girl thing to worry about, but it's the first thing that sprang to my mind, despite the outfit being out of my comfort zone.

"Oh, don't worry. You can wear it later... for me."

He types out a quick text and puts his phone away before facing me. "Now, where were we?"

"You wanted me to hear you out about something."

"Ah, right. I'll start with that text."

"Okay."

"Like I said before, you read it. You have to know that this isn't just going to be a matter of winning a court case. There's potentially real danger at your doorstep."

"I did read it, but it was just a text. Nothing else has happened. Right?"

"No, not yet," he concedes. "But trust me when I say this is going to get ugly. I've been a Soulless King long enough to know that nothing is what it seems on the surface. First it's a menacing text, and then it's an all-out war."

"You can't possibly know that."

"Yeah, Lexi. I can. I've experienced it. Over and over and over again, the Soulless Kings have fought to protect what's theirs. We always win, but that doesn't mean it doesn't get ugly along the way.

"So it might get ugly. What does that have to do with me?"

"Well, during our meeting with the club, Sling had a really good point."

"And that is?"

"We haven't been looking at the big picture."

"I'm pretty sure you being charged with murder is the big picture."

Squirrel shakes his head. "No, it's not. The club is. All of this points back to someone who has a grudge against the Soulless Kings, for whatever reason. We have to get back on our own turf so we can figure out what that reason is and take care of it."

"So if we turn in the tape, what about all those who took the bribe?"

"They'll get whatever punishment the criminal justice system wants to throw at them."

"And you're okay with that?"

"I have to be."

"Okay, let's say this all plays out the way you want it to. Those accepting bribes are held responsible. Then what? You go back to Oregon, and I stay here and flounder?"

Fury starts to settle in at the fact that the Soulless Kings, *Squirrel*, seems to be forgetting that I just quit my job for them. I put up the closed sign on my old life and took a chance on hanging an open sign on a life they thrust me into.

"No, not exactly."

I shoot up from the couch, startling Bug in the process, and begin to pace.

"Dammit, Squirrel, just spit it out. This is getting ridiculous."

He slowly rises and takes a deep breath. "You'd come to Oregon with us. With me."

My steps falter and I shake my head. "No. That's crazy. I can't do that."

"Why not? You were considering it anyway after the case was over. We're just moving the timeline up a bit."

*Touché.*

"Why would I have to go to Oregon? What's the reason beyond working for the club?" I pause and raise a brow. "Which, by the way, makes no sense because I haven't proven myself worth of that yet, at least as far as the contract is concerned. Shit, I haven't even spoken to your other attorney. What does he say about all of this?"

My questions come out disjointed and in rapid fire. Squirrel walks toward me and grips my upper arms to stop me from wearing a hole in the floor.

"Don't worry about Alan. He talked himself out of a job anyway. As for why you'd have to come to Oregon…"

"What? Spit it out."

"It's the only way I can make sure you stay above ground."

# Chapter Eighteen

*Everyone has a price.*

**Squirrel**

*Two weeks later...*

"In light of new evidence brought to me by Attorney Cantor and the defense team, the charges against Travis Kramer are dismissed, with the sincerest apologies of the court."

Sitting in the chair next to Lexi, with Alan Forney on the other side, I listen to Judge Belmont tell me I'm a free man. The courtroom becomes a mixture of cheers on my side and disdain from the family and friends of Maria Sampson. I wish they knew the full extent of what those in a position of power have done to thwart justice for Maria, but they will soon enough. It's bound to be plastered all over every newspaper and television screen. Not to mention, another prosecutor is going to have to keep them informed.

All Lexi had to do to get the trial moved up was let Judge Benton hear the tape of Firth admitting that he knew

I was innocent and that he was receiving a bribe to bring me down. With the help of a special prosecutor, it was decided to go forward with the trial, at least on the surface. Firth very much thought he was coming in here today to present a case and get me locked up.

*Joke's on him.*

Judge Benton bangs her gavel several times, trying to bring order to the courtroom. Firth rants and raves from behind the prosecution table, forcing the judge to shout.

"Mr. Firth, shut. Up."

I glance over at him and can see the sheen of sweat on his forehead, the way his hands are shaking. He looks toward our table, and his face turns red, but he finally does as he's told.

"I don't normally do this, but since I already dismissed the charges, and with the permission of the District Attorney, I would like the court to hear something."

I'm not sure where the speakers are, but Mr. Firth's voice is loud and clear as the tape is played for all in attendance. Shocked gasps and muffled tears can be heard underneath it all.

When the tape ends, the judge again looks to Firth. Before she can speak, he jumps to his feet.

"Your Honor, I can explain," he insists, panic in his voice.

"I highly doubt that Mr. Firth," she retorts, a look of disdain on her face. "In all the years I've been on this bench, I have never encountered a man as unscrupulous as you sitting at that particular table."

I love how she uses that qualifier—'that particular table'—because it conveniently excludes her and the bribe she took. She may be doing the right thing now, but she's not innocent either.

"Not only were you going to put an innocent man in prison for the rest of his natural life, but you were also going to let the Sampson family and all of Maria's loved ones believe her killer was caught."

"Your Honor, it's not what it—"

"I'm not done," she snaps. Firth closes his mouth, a dejected look on his face. "Now, I have already contacted the State Bar Association, and an investigation into your actions is forthcoming. Charges have already been filed against you by the District Attorney, and you will be remanded into custody until your arraignment hearing."

The bailiff handcuffs Mr. Firth, but he doesn't go quietly. As he's being led from the courtroom, he shouts, "You'll regret this! There are people involved and they won't stop. You'll regret it, I promise you!"

When he's fully removed from the room and Judge Benton once again calls order to the court, she lets her attention fall on the victim's family.

"I cannot begin to understand your grief, losing a child so young, so horrifically. I am truly sorry for your loss." She softens her expression and smiles sadly. "As one who prides herself at punishing crimes against children, I can only imagine how angry you must be today. And I am sorry for the role I am playing in causing that anger. But the justice system isn't meant to be a platform for witch hunts. I want Maria's killer brought to justice as much as you do. That being said, I am confident that, with new detective work and fresh eyes on the case, that can be accomplished."

Judge Benton leans forward, steepling her hands. "Before court adjourns, I want to address everyone in attendance." Her face returns to an impassive expression. "Let this be a lesson to all of you. Individuals are innocent until proven guilty for a reason. You might not like it, but it *can* work. Admittedly, not always, but when done right, it can. Court is adjourned."

She bangs the gavel, and the courtroom erupts into chaos. Reporters surge forward, some toward the family, and others toward me. Lexi expertly denies requests for any interviews with me, and I'm reminded why I wanted her to represent me.

The family, however, isn't so lucky as to have someone to act as a buffer.

Until the Soulless Kings step in. Within seconds, the brothers in attendance weave their way through the crowd and surround the family. They guide them toward the exit, but don't get far. A bailiff stops them and hands the mother a slip of paper. She opens it, and her eyes widen, but she nods.

The bailiff then walks in our direction. When he reaches our table, he stretches a hand out to me.

"I'm glad things worked out," he says as we shake hands. "I've seen some crazy stuff, but this takes the cake." Then his face lights up in a grin. "I'm just glad I didn't buy into Firth's fantasy football league. Shady bastard."

I can't help but laugh. "He is that."

"Anyway, the judge is requesting you and Miss Cantor in her chambers."

"Do you know what this is about?" Lexi asks.

"No ma'am. Just that she wants to talk to you both and the family together."

"Thank you for letting us know. We'll head that way now."

"No problem." He gives a polite nod. "Have a good day."

After he walks away, Lexi lifts her head to look at me and all I can do is shrug.

"This ought to be interesting," I say, as uneasy about this as Lexi seems to be.

I turn to Alan, who's standing behind me. "Let the others know where we are and that we'll meet them back at the clubhouse."

"I'm going with you," he bristles.

"No, Alan, you're not." Lexi steps in between us. "You couldn't be bothered to be here until last night, despite my efforts to get you here two weeks ago. I understand you're upset that Squirrel and the club chose me to handle this case, but it wasn't about you. I have done everything up until this point, I think I can handle a meeting with the judge. Your services are no longer required."

Alan blusters and his eyes dart from me to her and back again. "She can't do that. Tell her, Squirrel. It's not up to her to dismiss me."

Having already discussed Forney's future with the Soulless Kings and voted on it with members, I feel confident in my reply.

"I believe she already did it." Alan opens his mouth to speak, but I continue so fast, he slams it shut. "Now do what you're told before you make things worse for yourself."

Effectively dismissed, Alan sulks away, but not without mumbling under his breath. I can't make out what he says, but I really don't try. He's not worth the energy. Besides, I'm too keyed up about what the judge wants to care.

"Shall we?" I ask Lexi, looking down at her while she gathers her things.

"Let's do this."

## *Squirrel*

"Like so many things today, I don't normally do this," Judge Benton says, addressing Lexi, me, and Maria Sampson's mother and father. "But I felt it was too important."

We waited for the judge for almost an hour. Sitting in a cramped room with the family was awkward, and all I wanted to do was get out of this stupid suit. Now that we're finally standing in front of her, I still want out of it, but it's a little further from my mind.

"Mr. and Mrs. Sampson, your trust in the system, from the bottom to the top, must be at an all-time low."

"Yes, ma'am," Mrs. Sampson says quietly. She and her husband are sitting in the only two other chairs in the room other than the judge's. She's wringing her hands in her lap, and every few minutes, wiping tears from her face or blowing her nose. "They failed my baby."

"Our baby," Mr. Sampson says more forcefully. "How are we supposed to trust anyone? The cops don't care about our daughter. They never have."

Judge Benton nods. "I took the time to look through your daughter's juvenile records. I understand she was on probation at the time of her death. History of drugs, underage prostitution."

Mrs. Sampson sniffles. "We tried everything we knew to help her." Mr. Sampson rests his arm on his wife's thigh, and she grabs it like a lifeline. "When my husband lost his job, Maria was eight. Up until then, life was good. But then we had to move to a cheaper neighborhood, and she fell in with the wrong crowd."

"That's the impression I got when I looked at everything." Judge Benton's voice is soothing, non-judgmental. "As I said in the courtroom, I can't imagine what you are going through, but I would like to help."

"How can you help?" Mr. Sampson asks, clearly not trusting her. "No one could help before. What makes things different now?"

"The difference now is him." Judge Benton points to me.

Confusion settles in, and I look at Lexi, whose wrinkled brow tells me we're on the same page.

"I'm sorry, Your Honor, but how does my client factor in?"

"Miss Cantor, there's a reason you were asked to leave your cell phones outside my office before entering. What I'm about to say is off the record, and I will deny it until my dying day."

I thought it had been strange when a guard was standing outside the judge's chambers and collected all cell phones or any other electronic devices we each had before we were permitted entry.

"As it has so clearly been demonstrated in this case, the justice system isn't perfect." The judge speaks with authority, but also compassion. "It fails, and sometimes that failure marks cases with a black stain that they can never remove. I believe that this case is solvable, that the police probably even have an idea of who did it. But after today, I don't trust that they will do the right thing."

"What are you saying?" Mr. Sampson asks, impatience infusing his tone. "That my daughter will never get justice?"

"That's not what I'm saying at all, Mr. Sampson," she tells him. "But I am saying that justice may need to be procured in a more... *non-traditional* way." Judge Benton shifts her eyes to me. "That, Mr. Kramer, is where you and your club come in."

"I'm listening."

"I have a proposition for you. But first, I need to know that you are able to make decisions without putting it to a vote with the other members of your club." When I raise a brow at her, she adds. "I did my homework, Mr. Kramer. I know you're bound by certain rules as well as I am."

"Okay." I may be confused, but the more the judge speaks, the more and more I like her. "Depending on what it is, yes, I have the authority."

*At least, I hope.*

"Perfect." She clasps her hands. "Like you, I have connections. I'm willing to trade favors, if that's something you'd be open to."

"This is highly inappropriate, Your Honor," Lexi accuses, ever the rule follower.

"Yes, Miss Cantor, it is," Judge Benton agrees. "But what is worse? Doing what it takes to make sure Maria Sampson's killer is caught and punished, or letting a child killer remain free? And before you answer, I'll remind you that you gave up your job, potentially ruined your career to, I assume, do the right thing."

Lexi looks at me, her eyes pleading with me. To do what, I don't know. I know this puts her in an awful position, but it also serves as an eye opener to the world she's entering.

"What favors are you suggesting?" Lexi finally asks.

"It's my understanding, based on that tape, as well as information I've gathered by asking the right people certain questions, that Mr. Kramer, you're still being investigated by the FBI?"

"That's my understanding," I admit. "Although no charges have been filed that I'm aware of."

"Well, what I'm willing to do is use my connections to shut that investigation down."

"So, he's not a killer, but he's still a criminal?" Mr. Sampson bellows, rising from his chair. "And you're going to help him get away with it all?"

"Yes, Mr. Sampson," she replies. "That's exactly what I'm going to do. In exchange for justice for Maria, wouldn't you do the same?"

Mr. Sampson sits, his shoulders deflating. This has to be hard for him, for his wife.

"Sorry," he mumbles, referring to his outburst.

"No apology necessary," Judge Benton says. "Emotions are running high." She looks back at me. "Mr. Kramer, if I can get you off the hook with the feds, are you and the Soulless Kings willing to help the Sampson's get justice for their daughter?" She arches a brow. "No matter what it takes?"

"Yes, ma'am," I respond without hesitation.

"Now, wait," Lexi says. "I think my client and I need to take a minute to talk this—"

"I don't need a minute, Lexi. It's an easy decision." I walk to the side of the judge's desk and face Mr. and Mrs. Sampson. "I am sorry about what happened to your daughter. I wouldn't wish that on any family. But I can help you, my club can help you."

"Understand," Judge Benton interjects. "If you get the justice you want, it will likely be outside the confines of the law. You have to be willing to turn a blind eye to what it takes to accomplish your goal."

Mr. and Mrs. Sampson exchange a look before turning back to the judge and nodding. "We're fine with whatever it takes. As long as the person responsible pays."

"They'll pay," I say, renewed rage taking over at the thought of what Maria went through. "I promise you, they'll pay."

They both nod.

## Squirrel

"Good. Then it's settled. Before you leave, make sure to exchange information so you can keep in contact. Mr. and Mrs. Sampson, know that the police will still be conducting their investigation. I can't stop them from that, even if they've lost my faith in them. You cannot tell them what we have discussed or give any indication that there is an independent investigation going on."

"We understand," they say in unison.

"Okay. I appreciate you meeting with me. And again, my condolences on your loss. I wish you luck."

Knowing that their time in the judge's chambers is over, the Sampsons quietly thank the judge and me and depart the office. As soon as the door closes, Judge Benton stands and crosses her arms over her chest.

"Mr. Kramer, I don't like being put in the position I was put in by your club." I know she's referring to the bribe to grant me bail, but I stay quiet, sensing she's got more to say. "But knowing what I know now, I'm glad I took it."

"Me too."

Lexi remains silent beside me, seemingly taking it all in. I can only imagine how angry she is, and no doubt, her confidence will come back the moment we're clear of courthouse property. Then I'll get her wrath.

"You must know that stopping the FBI's investigation doesn't mean I stop whoever is behind this, whoever the original bribe came from."

"I do."

"I hope you can figure this out, stop the man, or woman, responsible."

"Oh, we will. Trust me. We won't stop until we do."

"Just don't forget about Maria. As easily as I can stop the investigation, I can get it started back up. You might not have a recording of this meeting because I made sure of that. But that doesn't mean that one doesn't exist."

*Damn. I didn't see that coming.*

"Understood."

"Good luck, Mr. Kramer." Judge Benton turns to Lexi. "As for you, Miss Cantor, I'm impressed. Not many young lawyers would do what you did. I certainly wouldn't have at your age."

Stunned, Lexi says, "I did what I thought was right."

"I know, which is why I'm going to give you a little piece of free advice." She pauses, takes a deep breath. "We come out of law school, bright-eyed and ready to take on all the injustices in the world. We have good intentions, but it's not always that easy. You chose to trust your gut this time. Keep doing that. Keep fighting for those who need it. Even if that means sometimes crossing a line you never thought you'd cross."

"I..." Lexi nods. "I will."

Judge Benton nods as if concluding her dispersion of words of wisdom. "Now, go. I have some phone calls to make." She locks her eyes on me. "Mr. Kramer, it turns out your friends were right."

"Your Honor?"

"Everyone has a price... even you."

# Chapter Nineteen

*I choose to keep putting my trust, and my life, in Squirrel's hands.*

**Lexi**

"I can't believe you're leaving."

I hug Courtney, and then Steph. They came to the rental house, the one that I'm now moving out of, to help load up the moving truck. I've only lived here a few weeks, and with the trial and potentially moving to Oregon looming, I never really let myself feel like it was home. Which is good, because it makes today so much easier.

"I know. But I'll be back," I assure them. "This whole Oregon thing might not work out." I worry my bottom lip. "That is if we even make it."

Squirrel has made sure to remind me, over and over, how much danger is out there, especially since we don't know who the bad guys are.

"You'll get there," Steph assures me. "You're in good hands. Squirrel and the others aren't going to let anything happen to you. I mean, isn't that why you agreed to go? For your safety?"

"Well, yeah." Among other things. "But they don't even know who the enemy is. It's a faceless person and could be anybody."

"That's true, but the Soulless Kings rarely know exactly who the enemy is at first. They'll figure it out, and when they do, you and Squirrel can go from there." Courtney winks. "In the meantime, enjoy his company, girl. I know if he hadn't already set his eyes on you, I'd be working on him." Her face falls. "And there's the distance thing. Can't exactly bang a guy when he's in a different state."

Jealousy hits me fast and hard. Squirrel and I have only shared that one kiss. Not because either of us didn't want to explore more, but because there hasn't been any opportunity. Things have been a whirlwind since the Soulless Kings and I made the decision to take the tape to the judge. Hell, it's only been two days since Squirrel made that deal with the judge.

And things aren't likely to settle down any time soon. Maybe the two of us are only destined to be friends but moving to Oregon gives me the chance to figure that out. Especially since I can justify the move by telling myself it's for my safety and a chance at a solid career.

"You about ready, Lexi?" Squirrel steps up to my right. "We've got a long few days ahead of us."

"Yeah, I'm ready."

I give Steph and Courtney one last hug and then whistle for Bug.

"C'mon Bug, let's go," I call out.

Bug comes running from the side of the house and follows me to the moving truck. Squirrel lifts Bug into the

## Squirrel

cab and then helps me up before circling the vehicle and getting in the driver's side.

"You're doing the right thing," Squirrel says after starting the engine.

"I hope so."

Squirrel reaches over Bug, who has already laid down between us on the bench seat, and grabs my hand.

"Lexi, I know you're scared. And I know you might not truly understand why this is necessary, but I promise you, it is. I trusted you with my life. Now it's your turn to trust me with yours."

I hear his words and take comfort in them somehow. He's right. He trusted me. He even became my champion, fighting for me to fight for him. It's only fair to give him the same opportunity.

Settling into the seat, I lean against the window and watch as he pulls out of the driveway. Fender and Greaser are riding in front of us while Joker takes the rear. Squirrel's Harley is safely on the truck, strapped in to his satisfaction. We are also receiving an escort from the Michigan chapter of the Soulless Kings, at least as far as to the Michigan border.

The sound of Harley's surrounding us is deafening, but it's welcome. It makes me feel safer, like the world past all the metal doesn't exist, like nothing can penetrate the wall of bikers.

"Why don't you take a nap," Squirrel suggests. "You've gotta be exhausted." He ruffles Bugs fur. "He's got the right idea."

I shake my head. "I wanna stay awake."

"Mind if I turn the music on?"

"Not at all."

Squirrel turns the nob on the dash until he finds a rock

station that comes in. AC/DC fills the truck. We spend the next hour listening to the radio and talking about our mutual tastes in music. Once we tire of that, we move on to other topics that are just as safe: favorite foods, first kiss, hobbies... everything. And when we run out of safe things, I decide to take things to a more personal level.

"Tell me about your family."

He glances at me out of the corner of his eye. "You've met them. Well, some of them. You'll meet the rest when we get to Oregon."

"No, not them. Your real family."

"Lexi," he says with a hard tone. "The Soulless Kings are my real family."

"But what about your mom, your dad?"

I watch him carefully. His hands flex around the steering wheel, and his jaw hardens.

"Didn't you get all that info from your research?"

"I know what's in your file, Squirrel. And it doesn't match how you're reacting to the question. By all accounts, they were good parents. But I want to hear what you have to say."

"There's nothing to say." He shrugs. "My childhood was normal. No abuse or anything like that. I was a troublemaker, but they handled it well. But what they couldn't handle was me joining the Soulless Kings, and because of that, we haven't spoken in years."

I reach over and rest my hand on his arm. "I'm sorry."

"Nothing to be sorry for. They're good people, just not my people anymore."

"I get it. I mean, I told you about my parents. They, too, aren't bad people. Just unrealistic. And, I suppose, not my people. At least not in the way I would like."

Squirrel takes a deep breath and squeezes my hand

before letting both go. "And now, like me, you'll have the Soulless Kings as family."

"See, that doesn't make sense to me," I tell him.

He chuckles. "In case you don't know it yet, I like you. That's all it takes for them to embrace you."

"But that doesn't equate to family."

"No, I suppose it normally wouldn't. But it's different with an MC. Once someone is brought into the fold, they're accepted as one of our own. Especially when it comes to a woman a brother has staked a claim on."

"You've staked a claim on me?"

*This is news to me. I don't know how I feel about it.*

"If you're asking if I told them all to back the fuck off because you're mine, yes." He nods. "But if you're asking if I believe you're mine in the sense that I own you or will force you into a relationship you don't want, no." He quickly glances at me, his face serious. "I wouldn't do that."

*Okay. I kinda like it.*

"I can live with that."

"So, are you saying you like me too?"

I twist in my seat to face him. "Squirrel, I wouldn't be moving to Oregon if I didn't like you. Not even for a career opportunity. I still feel like we have a lot to learn about each other. You have this entire life that I have yet to see."

"I can live with that," he mimics my words.

I have more questions for him... so many more. I just don't know if I should ask them, especially when I have no way to escape him if I don't like the answers. But apparently, I can't help myself.

"Have you ever killed anyone?"

"Yes," he responds without hesitation.

My heart skips a beat. My head knew the answer before

the question was out of my mouth, but my heart was hoping I was wrong.

"Who?"

"I can't tell you." He reaches out to turn the radio off. "But I promise, it wasn't a situation like with Maria Sampson."

I think about that for a minute and realize I'm not as upset by the information as I thought I'd be.

*Huh.*

"How did you kill them?"

"You don't want to know."

"Yeah, Squirrel, I do."

"Lexi, trust me. It's not a pretty story. None of them are."

"So you've killed more than once?"

"Yes."

"Oh."

"Listen, I'm the tech guy for the Soulless Kings. I'm normally not on the front lines of the fighting, but that doesn't mean I won't step up when I'm needed. I don't regret it. I'll never regret it. It's a part of being a Soulless King, and I love my life and what we do."

"The drug business?" I ask tentatively. When he gives me a questioning look, I shrug. "Research."

"That's part of it. But there's so much more. We take out bad people."

"And in the process, forget that what you're doing illegally is also bad?"

"No." Squirrel shakes his head. "We don't deny who we are. We don't pretend to be something we're not."

I think back to when members circled the Sampsons in the courtroom. He's right. They don't put on a show or pretend to be people they aren't. Every single one of them was wearing his cut, proudly displaying who they were. But there's heart there.

And that matters.

"My turn to ask a question," he says, breaking me free of my thoughts.

"Go for it."

"Did you tell your parents you were moving to Oregon?"

Air rushes past my lips, and my shoulders deflate. "You know I haven't."

"Don't you think you should?"

"Why? So they can tell me all the reasons they're disappointed in my choices, yet again?" I shake my head. "No thank you."

"Lexi, you need to tell them," he insists. "What if something goes wrong?"

"I thought you said I would be safe by going with you."

Squirrel nods. "Yeah, you are." He sighs. "You should still tell them."

I shift so I'm facing forward again, wanting to end the conversation. I look out the window, and in the rearview mirror, I see that only Joker remains behind us. I don't know when we left Michigan, but I missed it.

Squirrel's words play in my mind: What if something goes wrong? That's a hell of a question. What if? The answer is, I just don't know. I can't control what happens or how it all ends. But I can control how I proceed until then.

And I choose to keep putting my trust, and my life, in Squirrel's hands.

# Chapter Twenty

*Ah, home*

**Squirrel**

"Welcome back!"

Royal jumps down from his stool in the gate house and up to the truck. I rolled the window down about an hour ago, grateful to be breathing in Oregon air. It feels like a lifetime has passed since I was hauled away from here, but finally, I'm home.

"Hey, brother." I pull him through the window for an awkward bear hug. "How are things here?"

"Same old, same old."

"Chaos and mayhem, then." I chuckle. "Good to know some things never change."

Royal's eyes shift from me to Lexi. "And who do we have here?" He whistles. He's lucky I know he's harmless, or his neck would be snapped in two. "This must be the famous lawyer lady."

"Watch it, Royal." I glance over my shoulder. "Lexi, this is Royal. He's a pain in the ass, but harmless."

"Nice to meet you."

"You too, Lexi."

We talk for a few more minutes before I drive the moving truck the rest of the way up the drive to the clubhouse. Most of Lexi's belongings will be stored in a part of the basement that's separate from the Nightmare Room. She'll be staying with me until we figure out who blackmailed the authorities. Once that's done, and I know she'll be safe, I'll help her find a place to live.

"Do you mind if we stop here real quick so I can say hi to everyone?" I ask her. "Then we can head to my place."

"No, I don't mind. I'd like to meet them all."

I jump out of the truck and rush around to help her down to the ground. Bug jumps out after her and takes off to a tree to hike his leg.

"Is he going to be okay coming inside?" Lexi asks.

"I told you, the guys are gonna love him. Not to mention the ol' ladies. He'll be fine."

"Okay. Should I put him on a leash?"

"Nah."

I lead her inside, Bug on our heels, and when we breach the threshold, she hesitates. The main room of the clubhouse is filled to capacity. Everyone is here. Riker, Piston, Trainwreck... their significant others. All the prospects, numerous Bangin' Betties, friends of the club. Even Alan Forney is sitting at the bar holding a tumbler of amber liquid.

I press my hand to the small of her back as I lean in close to her. "It's okay. No one bites... unless you ask them to." Lexi nods but doesn't relax. "I'll make it quick."

"You sure are a sight for sore eyes," Piston says as he rushes me and lifts me in a bear hug.

My hand falls away from Lexi as a result, but as soon as he sets me back on my feet, I grab her hand.

"Tell me about it," I say to him. "Piston, this is Lexi. The genius who got me home."

"I've heard a lot about you, Lexi." He gives her a hug and a little squeak escapes her as he does.

"Oh." She pushes her glasses up her nose and smiles. "All good I hope."

"Absolutely. Welcome to our clubhouse."

"Thank you."

Trainwreck pushes past Piston, and his grin spreads from ear to ear. "Jesus, you had to make my day all about you, didn't you?"

Sylvia sidles up next to him. "What he said."

"I know it's a little late, but congratulations." I hug Sylvia. "I'm happy for you two."

"Thank you, Squirrel." Sylvia smiles at me and then looks at Lexi and introduces herself. "This idiot got himself arrested the night we got engaged."

"Damn," Lexi mutters.

"Thank you for getting him back to us," Trainwreck says."

"Fuck, bro, you're acting like you were never gonna see me again," I snap with humor.

"Ya never know around here."

"Dude, don't scare her away," I joke, giving Lexi a smile so she knows we're only messing around.

*Are you though?*

"I'll stop hogging your time. Everyone else wants to see your ugly ass and meet her." Trainwreck nods at Lexi.

He and Sylvia walk away and mingle through the

## Squirrel

crowd. It takes more time than I'd like to introduce her to everyone, but she's a trooper. After meeting the ol' ladies, she tries to hide a yawn behind her hand.

"Why don't we get to my place?" I say, steering her toward the door. "I'm beat."

It's a lie. I'm home, with my brothers, and I want to hang out. But I won't if she needs to rest.

"If you're sure," she says.

I push open the door and step out into the dark night. We were inside much longer than I anticipated.

"Thanks for letting me stop and say hey to everyone."

"Squirrel, you don't need to thank me. It's clear that you all love each other. I'm just glad we were able to get you home."

*Home.*

It's such a weird word. When you're little, you're taught that home is a place, whether it be a house, an apartment, or even a houseboat. But as you get older, that definition blurs, morphs until you don't recognize it. Not that it's unrecognizable. More like, different.

In your teens, and sometimes even into your early twenties, you tend not to understand or grasp why home looks different, feels different. And in some cases, that feeling remains. But in other cases, like mine, you're able to put your finger on the difference.

Home isn't a place... it's a feeling. It's the people you surround yourself with.

The Soulless Kings are home.

I lock eyes with Lexi.

And now, so is she.

I grab her hand and guide her to the back of the moving truck. As I open the latch, Lexi stands to the side, watching.

"We're not unloading this now, are we?"

"Not a chance in hell."

"Then what are you doing?"

Rather than answer, I walk up the ramp and unstrap my Harley. I ease it off the truck, and when I lower the kickstand, I just stand there.

To some, it's a hunk of metal, a death trap. To me, it's the last piece to make my home complete.

"Squirrel, I don't know if I can drive this thing," Lexi says, nodding at the truck. "It's dark, I'm tired. Can't you ride that to your place tomorrow?"

"Oh, you're not driving the truck." I swing my leg over the seat. "You're riding with me."

I didn't have many opportunities to ride in Michigan and definitely none where she was able to go with me.

She feverishly shakes her head. "I don't think so."

I reach my hand out, palm up. "Do you trust me?"

She crosses her arms over her chest. "Are we really going there again?"

I shrug.

"Squirrel, it's not about—"

"Lexi, please." I lower my head before lifting it again and locking eyes with hers. "I need this."

She hesitates, deals with her glasses, and then heaves a sigh. Lexi takes a tentative step forward and slaps her hand into mine. When she settles against my back, her arms around my waist, a peace I haven't felt in weeks settles over me.

*Ah, home.*

# Chapter Twenty-One

*What would it be like to have him funnel all that energy into... me?*

**Lexi**

Sun streams through the window, bouncing rays off the screen of my cell phone, making the words hard to see. It doesn't matter. They're engraved on my brain, right into the gray matter.

**Don't get too comfortable. You may have won Squirrel this round, but I'm not finished yet.**

How did this happen? How did this person get my number? When I took the job at the public defender's office, I took measures to make sure that my number was unlisted and there were safeguards in place so it didn't get out.

*You left the public defender's office, remember?*

How could I forget?

I make my way to the bathroom off the hallway,

listening for sounds that Squirrel is awake. Noise comes from the kitchen, and seconds later, the smell of coffee reaches my nose. I close my eyes in appreciation, but then my bladder reminds me of why I got out of bed.

After I finish in the bathroom, I return to the spare bedroom and flop down on the bed. These are the times when I wish I had someone I could call, someone I trusted, someone to run ideas by. Ya know? All the things most people call their friends about.

I lift my phone off the mattress again to look at the text. As I reread the words, my stomach churns because I realize that, as much as I don't want to show Squirrel, he's also the *only* person I want to show. Not just because he needs to know, but because he kind of checks all those boxes that friends check.

Without bothering to change into something more decent than my light pink shorts and tank, I pad to the kitchen, phone in hand.

"Glad you could join—"

Squirrel turns around with a coffee mug in his hand and freezes. I glance down at myself, wondering what he's staring at, but I can't figure it out.

"What?" I ask.

He shakes his head and hands me the mug. "That's exactly what you were wearing the day I showed up at your apartment. Minus the hoodie, though." He smirks.

I look down again and see that my nipples are showing. Heat burns my cheeks, but unfortunately, the embarrassment does nothing to tone down the headlights.

"Cold?"

"Shut up," I snap before taking a sip of coffee. I moan at its caffeinated goodness.

"I like the sound of that."

"I've slept in your house for one night, and already that starts?" I taunt.

I don't know why I'm feeding into it, but it feels good, this playful banter. Much better than what's coming after I show him the text.

"The first of many nights," he teases right back. He turns to refill his own mug but continues talking. "So, how'd you sleep?"

"Good." I pull out a chair at the round table and sit. "You?"

"Like a baby."

Squirrel takes the seat opposite me, but his eyes never leave my face.

"You okay?" he asks, one brow raised.

I've never been good at lying, so I don't even try. I pull up the text and set my phone on the table to slide it toward him.

"I woke up to that."

Squirrel's jaw hardens and his fist clenches around his mug. Before I know what's happening, the mug shatters against the wall, falling to pieces on the floor.

"Motherfucker!" he shouts, running his fingers through his hair.

I watch as he paces for a few minutes, muttering to himself as if he's trying to figure out the world's problems on his own. Then he stomps off to the door that leads to the basement. He yanks it open, and his footsteps on the rickety wood echo up to me.

When he gave me the 'nickel tour' last night, he didn't take me down there, but he did tell me it's where he works, so I assume it's where all his computer equipment is.

Deciding he needs a few minutes to cool down, I clean up the broken glass, depositing it all in the trash. Then I make my way down to see what he's doing, and when I reach the bottom step, my jaw drops.

Laid out in an almost horseshoe pattern is what I would describe as a war room. Monitor after monitor line two of the walls, while the third is a giant whiteboard. There's only one chair, and Squirrel is in it. Obviously, he likes to work alone.

Too bad. He brought me here, into this house, so he's not alone.

"Go back upstairs," he commands without looking at me.

"No."

"Lexi, I can't fucking be around you right now. I'm too pissed off, and I have shit to do."

I remain where I am for what feels like an eternity, waiting for him to stand up and bodily remove me from the room, but he doesn't. Instead, he remains focused on his task, whatever that might be.

I take the opportunity to stare. As he types, I can see the muscles in his bare forearms flex under his skin. His shoulders strain against his T-shirt. His leg bounces under the desk, evidence of his pent-up energy.

As I take a few steps toward him, I breathe deeply, and admire the physical perfection that he is. It's not as if I haven't noticed his looks before but seeing him in what is clearly his element drives home how sexy he is.

Squirrel is confident here, assured of his every move. He was in Michigan too, but it was different.

"What can I do to help?" I ask when I'm standing right behind him.

*Squirrel*

He tips his head back to look at me, his face a mask of rage and determination. "Nothing. Go back upstairs."

"Already told you I'm not doing that. So you might as well put me to use."

Squirrel heaves a sigh.

"Here." He hands me my cell phone. I stare at it like it's going to burn me if I touch it. "Take it."

"Why?"

"Because I want to try something."

I lift the phone into my hand. "Okay."

"See that screen there?" he asks as he points to the one just to his left. "See how the map is blank?"

"Yes."

He points to the monitor to his right. "And then there's this one, with that little red dot."

"Uh huh."

"This dot is you. It's remaining still because you aren't moving." He twists to look at the left screen. "You're going to text this asshole back, and hopefully, with the code I put into your phone, we can trace him if he responds. He'll show up on this screen."

Nerves settle into my stomach. "I can't do that. What in the hell do I say?"

"Anything, Lexi. Just bait him. Maybe he'll even give away little details in his responses."

"And if you can track him, what then?"

"I take the info to the club, and we go get him, find out why the fuck he's doing this."

"Right."

Breathing deeply, I pull up the text app on my phone. My fingers hover over the screen as I try to think of what to type. I decide on simple.

**Who is this?**

I shift my gaze from my cell to the monitors Squirrel is focused on and see that he's
mirroring my phone so he can watch what I type. Somehow, that makes me feel a little better.

Squirrel taps away at the keyboard in front of him while we wait for a response. Fortunately, we don't have to wait long.

**If I told you, that would take all the fun out of this, now wouldn't it?**

"Fucker thinks this is a game," Squirrel growls.
"Obviously," I say, my voice a little shaky. "Now what?"
"Keep going. One text isn't going to do it. You've got his attention, use it... Balls."
The taunt does what he no doubt intended it to do: gives me a boost in confidence. He's right. If I can do what I've done in the last few weeks, I can maintain a text conversation.

**Me: This is fun to you?**

**Him: As fun as mayhem is to the Soulless Kings.**

"You were right, Squirrel. This is about the club."
"I know. Keep going."

**Me: What did they do to you?**

*Squirrel*

**Him: Wouldn't you like to know?**

**Me: Yes.**

**Him: Let's just say they took something from me.**

**Me: Okay. And having Squirrel in prison for life would have given you that something back?**

**Him: No. But revenge feels good.**

"Squirrel, he's not going to give anything away."

Pings fill the room, and my eyes dart to the screen that's supposed to track this guy.

There are little red dots littering the map.

"He doesn't have to. The code is working."

"How?" I cry. "There's dozens of those location dots. It's not exactly narrowing things down."

"He's bouncing off different IP addresses, which tells me his phone is connected to Wi-Fi or he's using a computer-based texting program."

"So? I'm still not clear how you're getting what you want out of this."

"Think about it, Lexi. We can rule out anything outside the US. He's not going to set all this up and not be close to watch it play out."

"Are you sure? Because that's exactly what I would do in his shoes. Set it up and then get the hell out of dodge."

Squirrel leans back in his chair and links his hands behind his head.

"I suppose it's a possibility, but I don't think that's what he's doing."

Without thinking, I rest my hand on his arm, and my palm tingles at the contact. I shudder and pray he doesn't feel it.

"Why do you think he's close?" I squeeze his arm. "Tell me why."

Squirrel stands from his chair and rolls it out of the way as he turns to face me.

"I just do, Lexi." His eyes seem to stare straight through me, right into my soul. There's an imploring quality to them. "I can't explain it. I just feel it in my gut. This piece of shit isn't far."

We stare at one another for a beat longer before I nod. "Okay." I lift the phone back up. "What should I say next?"

Squirrel starts pacing again, alternating between running his hands through his hair and over his chest. Heat pools in my stomach, lowering until it's ablaze between my thighs.

*Not the time, Lexi.*

Squirrel is the type of man you can't help but notice. He's tall, sexy, built like a brick wall. He's smart, funny... and so close I can touch him.

*Not the time, Lexi.*

What would it be like to have him funnel all that energy into... me?

"See if he'll open up about why he's targeting me," Squirrel says.

I lick my lips, fully aware that I was going down a rabbit hole that neither of us have time for right this second.

"Right. Um, okay."

**Me: So you want revenge against Squirrel?**

*Squirrel*

**Him: Yes. And the others.**

**Me: Why Squirrel?**

**Him: Because his particular skills made it possible for the rest of them to take something from me.**

"Your skills?" I ask, looking at Squirrel again. "I'm assuming he's talking about all this.

Any idea what he's referring to when he says the club took something from him?"

"Lexi, I've used my skills, as he calls them, to help the club with lots of things. This guy could be anyone from a lowlife down the street to a senator."

"I'm not even gonna ask."

"That's probably for the best. For now anyway."

I glance at the monitors and see that more location dots have popped up. This guy is good. I lean in close to count the ones that are local. If Squirrel is right, and he's close, we can narrow it down to thirteen locations instead of what is now hundreds. That's gotta be good, right?

"Don't you think it's time to call Fender?" I ask, knowing that he's not supposed to keep things from the club and not wanting him to get in trouble.

"I will." He reaches out a hand. "Give me your phone," he demands.

I hand it to him. He wastes no time tapping out a text. And it's seconds later when a response comes through.

"Son of a bitch!"

"What?"

Squirrel flips the phone around and once again, I'm reading words that make my blood run cold. Squirrel asked if any of the club members would recognize him if they saw him.

His response?

**Ask Alan Forney.**

# Chapter Twenty-Two

*To some, she's small and timid. But to me, she's a force of nature who doesn't back down from a challenge.*

**Squirrel**

Ask Alan Forney.

Ask Alan Forney.

Alan Forney, Alan Forney, Alan Forney.

My vision blurs, and a red haze swirls in front of me. What the fuck does that son of a bitch have to do with this?

"Squirrel?"

What does he know?

*Everything. Alan knows everything.*

He's been a good attorney. A great one in fact. Alan's been with the club for years, always doing whatever it takes to get us out of legal jams, out of jail, out of whatever is thrown our way.

*Until you needed him for a murder charge.*

No. This guy is bluffing. Trying to throw me off his trail.

"Squirrel?"

And if he's telling the truth? The club already plans to fire Forney. He fucked up in the way he talked to Fender, to me. And sure, maybe we were going to rough him up a bit. But he would have walked away. At least, that was the plan as far as I understood.

"Squirrel?!"

I whip my head up and see Lexi standing there, wringing her hands and wearing a worried expression. When I say nothing, she takes a tentative step toward me. I take a step back.

Her forehead crinkles, and hurt flashes in her eyes. The slap of her hands when she drops her arms to her sides echoes around me. She pulls her bottom lip in between her teeth and then runs her tongue over it.

My cock swells. I'm enraged beyond reason, and yet, I want her. I need her. Burying myself in her pussy would go a long way to calming me down.

But no. Lexi deserves better than that. I twist away from her and brace myself on the desk, arms stretched out.

"Squirrel, talk to me," she pleads from behind me.

Her voice washes over me like honey, trying to soothe me way down deep, but my fury won't let it penetrate.

"I need you to go upstairs, Lexi," I say with clenched teeth. "Now!"

My rage is too great for her. I would never forgive myself if I hurt her, and right now, I can't promise I won't. Not when I'm like this. I've never dealt with uncertainty well, and not knowing what to believe is sending me in a tailspin I don't want to take her on.

There's a reason I'm the tech guy of the club. A reason that goes way beyond being damn good at what I do.

I don't like to hurt people. Not like my brothers do.

## Squirrel

Don't get me wrong, I'll do what is necessary, and I'll kill when I have to. But I prefer not to.

But now? With Lexi involved? I'm craving violence like a mouse craves cheese. And I'm not so sure I can be discerning about who I hurt.

"Go. Upstairs."

A small hand settles on my back, and I know she's ignoring me. I really wish she wouldn't.

"No." Her voice is small and sounds far away.

I turn around and grip her wrists in one swift movement, exerting much more pressure than she deserves.

"I'm not going to tell—"

"You don't scare me, Squirrel."

"I should."

She shrugs. "Maybe. But you don't."

I stare at her, this woman who isn't running for the hills. To some, she's small and timid. But to me, she's a force of nature who doesn't back down from a challenge. One who will fight for what she wants, even when it might not be in her best interest.

I need that in my life. I need her.

She places her hand against my chest, and I glance at it, needing to see that it's real.

My dick twitches at her touch, at the way her eyes are pools of liquid fire. When she steps closer, so her body aligns with mine, I feel like I'll combust. With anger and lust riding double, I'm a powder keg.

She locks her eyes on mine and doesn't waver. Not when a low growl escapes past my lips. Not when my hands thread in her hair and tug. Not once does she second guess her decision to stay right here.

*Don't do it, man. She deserves better.*

Way past any ability to see reason, I bend and lift her

into my arms, crashing my lips to hers as I do. I back her against the whiteboard wall and assault her mouth. Our tongues meet, collide in a dance that is as old as time.

Lexi's hands find their way under my shirt, and I burn. Her fingertips trace a path up my stomach, over my pecs, until she digs her nails into my flesh.

"This is gonna be rough," I groan into her mouth.

Her nails dig in farther in response. I pin her to the wall and break the kiss long enough to reach down and pull her tank top up and over her head. I toss it to the floor and then add my shirt to it.

I lock eyes with her. Lexi's lips are swollen, her cheeks flushed. While I penetrate her with my gaze, I pull her shorts to the side and find her bare underneath, making it easy to slide my finger through her slick folds.

"You're wet and ready for me."

She nods.

"Use your words, Lexi. Tell me."

"Yes," she breathes. "I'm wet for you. Only you."

I set her on her feet and drop to my knees on the cement floor, yanking her shorts down as I do. I lift one of her legs over my shoulder and lean in to inhale her scent.

"Yeah you are."

I flatten my tongue against her clit and simultaneously penetrate her with two fingers. I waste no time doing what it takes to bring her to ecstasy. Her hands grab my head, holding me close.

I lap at her, eat her like a starving man. I circle her clit with my tongue, alternating directions, pressure, anything, everything. I twist my fingers so I'm touching her G-spot and tease her, torture her.

"Holy shit," she moans. "So good."

"Is this what you thought of in the shower that day?"

Her hips buck, matching the thrust of my fingers.

"Mmm."

"Come for me, baby."

I renew my resolve to throw her off that ledge. Her pussy is slick, warm, inviting, and I can't wait for my cock to experience it, but this orgasm is just for her.

When her hands leave my head and slap the wall, I know she's close. Her cunt spasms, once, twice, before clamping down. I use my free hand to steady her as her legs shake, her body quakes. And all because of what I'm doing to her.

Lexi's body relaxes, and I take a moment to appreciate her swollen, pink pussy before licking up the results of her pleasure. I slide up her now sweaty body, knowing I'm not done. That was for her. This next part is for me.

"You are delicious," I whisper as I trail kisses around her nipples, up over her collarbone.

"Mmm."

"If you think you're incapable of speech now," I taunt. "You just wait."

I shove my pants down to free my cock, and it slaps against my stomach. Lexi lowers her head, and her eyes widen when she gets her first look at me, at what is going to make her scream... in all the best ways.

"All for you, baby," I tell her.

Her eyes light up and she grins. "Good."

Without warning, she jumps up to wrap her legs around my waist. I catch her and make sure she steady against the wall before impaling her in one long stroke.

"So full," she moans, her head thrown back.

I thrust in and out of her at a pace I didn't know I could manage. I'm no saint and have fucked my share of women, but none have felt as incredible, as insanely perfect as Lexi.

I fuck her so fast, so hard that my muscles start to burn, almost as much as the rest of me. My hips fly, all my anger, lust, and energy being expended into one repetitive movement. I've lost all control, and if this is what it feels like, I'm not so sure I want it back.

"Harder, Squirrel. Fuck me harder," she demands.

Harder? I'm not sure how much harder I'm capable of. Not without hurting her. But I'll damn well try.

Primal. Unchecked. That's how I fuck this woman who, in a matter of weeks, has captivated me in a way that shouldn't be possible. That's how I fuck the woman who deserves more but wants me just as I am.

Lexi uses the wall for leverage, and she meets me thrust for thrust. Our bodies are in a rhythm that is impossible to break.

"Coming," she cries. "I'm coming!"

Her walls clamp down on my cock, and that's all it takes to fall over the edge with her. I shout out my release, as does she, and the sound echoes around us, surrounds us. My cock pulses and empties into her for what feels like forever, and it's amazing.

When it's over, I expect my dick to go limp, my body to give out. But it doesn't. As long as I'm inside of her, it'll never happen. She fuels me more than any anger ever could.

Lexi's head collapses against my chest. Our breathing is labored, each of us panting.

"That was unexpected."

Her words are muffled, but I hear them. And worry.

I pull out of her and set her on her feet before turning away and searching for my clothes. After I get dressed, I face her again. She's still naked, gleaming in the aftermath, but that hurt from earlier is back on her face.

*Squirrel*

"What's wrong, Squirrel?"

"Nothing."

She steps toward me and grabs my hand. "When I said that was unexpected, I didn't mean it in a bad way."

"You deserved better than being fucked in a basement by an animal."

"I deserved you, Squirrel. And I got you. The real you."

Is this woman real? Can she really mean what she says? I search her eyes for any signs that she's not being honest. I come up empty.

"I promise, next time will be different."

She arches a brow. "Next time?"

"Baby, now that I've had you, I'm gonna need more of you."

Lexi bends to pick up her clothes. She puts her glasses on, the ones I don't remember taking off.

"I like the sound of that."

# Chapter Twenty-Three

*We have one another's backs. Always have, always will.*

**Squirrel**

As much as I wanted to enjoy the aftermath with Lexi, my mind raced back to Alan Forney and what the hell to do about him. She seemed to understand that though, which is good. She's going to need to understand that a lot more often if she sticks around for any length of time.

*Forever, perhaps.*

I made a point to call Fender and ask him to get everyone together back at the clubhouse for church. I can't keep the texts from them, even if I still don't have any clue what they mean.

"Do you want me to write down every location, or just the ones within the state?"

I glance up from my own notes and look at her. "Just the ones in the state."

She nods before returning to the task at hand. We

## Squirrel

agreed that she would stay here while I go to the clubhouse, but she insisted on helping me get my ducks in a row before I go. I wanted to argue but thought better of it. She's an attorney and maybe she'll think of something I won't while we're compiling info. Not that there's much.

"Hey, look at this."

She turns her notebook for me to see. "What am I looking at?"

"See this address? I recognize it."

I narrow my eyes, trying to recall where the place is, but can't. If I don't know, how could she?"

"Where is it?" I ask her.

"It's an office space in town."

"Okay." I'm not real sure where she's going with this, or why the address is important.

"After I signed the contract, I did some digging. If there was potential for me to work in Oregon, I wanted to know what my options were."

"I'm not following."

She heaves a sigh, as if I'm being an idiot. "This is one of the spaces I checked out. As far as I know, it's an empty building, so how would someone be bouncing off an IP address that doesn't exist?"

Lexi runs her finger over her notes and her eyes widen. "In fact, several of these addresses are ones I looked up." She looks at me, confusion and fear warring for their place in her expression.

"I think you're right, and the buildings are empty. He's manipulating the addresses somehow, mirroring them or something. I don't know. I've never seen anything like it."

"Or maybe he's been to each of them," she says. "That makes more sense." She slaps me on the arm. "Think about it. He wouldn't have to gain entry into the buildings. Just secure a router or something to the outside."

"It's possible. I'll make sure we send someone to check it out."

"Squirrel?"

"What?"

"If I'm right, and this person has physically attached routers to these locations, that means he's closer than we realize."

I narrow my eyes. "I know."

"Right now, it's just a bunch of harmless texts, but what if..."

I pull Lexi into my lap and brush a strand of hair out of her face. "You're safe here. I promise. You've got me, all the security of the Soulless Kings. And let's not forget Bug. He's not gonna let anything happen to you."

Lexi's hands fly to her mouth. "Oh shit, Bug. I can't believe I forgot about him."

I grab her wrists and move her hands to her lap. "He's fine. I took him out this morning before you even got up. I made sure his food and water bowls were full. He was sacked out on the couch right before you came out into the kitchen. I'm sure he's still there."

Her shoulders sag with relief. "Thank you."

"You're welcome."

We spend the next half hour making sure I've got all the info I need to take to church. We return upstairs, and I take a quick shower. No need to let the guys smell the sex on me.

"I'm gonna head over to the clubhouse. Are you sure you don't wanna go?" I ask as I put on my cut while standing at the front door.

"I'm sure. I'm gonna get some of my stuff put away in my room, spend time curled up with Bug."

## Squirrel

"Okay. I shouldn't be too long. If you get bored, head over. I'm sure the ladies will be there."

"I'll be fine."

I debate on whether or not to kiss her goodbye. I stand there for a moment, unsure, unknowing if we've crossed that line into normal relationship stuff or if it was just sex and nothing more.

Throwing caution to the wind, I close the distance between us and place a kiss on her forehead. When she smiles, I know I made the right call.

"Be back soon."

"Uh huh."

I roll my eyes and race out the door, now running a few minutes late. I hop on my Harley and tear off for the clubhouse, not that it's far. But now that there's distance between Lexi and me, my focus isn't split. Now all I can think of is nailing the bastard that tried to ruin my life and is now trying to ruin the club.

"LET ME GET THIS STRAIGHT," FENDER SAYS, FURY IN his tone. "This guy, or bitch or whatever, is linking all of this to Alan?"

"That's what it looks like, Prez," I tell him.

It took me a while to lay out what I know for the club. They listened quietly while I tried to explain the code I embedded on Lexi's phone, how we tried to trap him. I could tell by their glazed expressions that they didn't understand the technical jargon, but they got the gist.

"I knew he seemed off," Joker seethes. "He just wasn't acting right when it came to the trial."

"Yeah, but how off?" Riker asks. "I wasn't there, so I

don't know, but maybe he just felt like he was being replaced."

"It's possible. And that's certainly how it came across," I admit. "He definitely didn't like Lexi taking over."

"Would you?" Piston counters. "I mean, we've employed him for years, and suddenly this chick shows up and takes over. I'd be pissed too."

"She's not just some chick," I snap, a little too forcefully. "She's damn good at her job, and me standing here is proof of that."

Piston holds up his hands. "Roger that. I'm not trying to step on your toes man, or talk down about her. Just laying out things as I think Alan might have seen them."

"Everyone just calm down," Fender says and stands from his chair. "Squirrel brought us some good information to start with." He glances around the table and stops when his eyes reach our most recent patched member. "Trainwreck, I want you to take Royal and go check out these addresses. See if anything looks out of the ordinary."

"You got it, Prez."

"Joker and Piston, I want the two of you to go to Alan's house. If he's there, grab him and bring him here. He can hang out in the Nightmare Room. If he's not, search the house, see if you can find anything suspicious... documents, bank records, anything that might help us narrow down if we should be worried about him."

"We can do that," Joker says.

"We're really going to put him in the Nightmare Room?" Piston questions.

"Why wouldn't we? He's a possible threat. We've taken out others for less."

"Not to be disrespectful, Prez," Piston begins. "But I

## Squirrel

think this is something that should be put to a vote. We always vote when it's someone this close to the club."

"Fine," Fender barks. "All those in favor of Alan going to the Nightmare Room?"

Half of the men around the table thump twice.

"All those in favor of nixing the Nightmare Room for now?"

The rest thump once.

"Are you fucking kidding me?" I explode, shoving up from my chair and sending it flying. "We've never hesitated to use that room any other time. Hell, many of you were on board with using it for Charlie. And if you'll recall, we did!"

"Squirrel," Fender growls, a menacing threat in his tone. "Watch it."

"All due respect, Prez, no. I was almost put into prison for life, labeled a child murderer." I take a deep breath. "And now this asshole is bringing Lexi into it. I won't watch it. There's too much at stake."

Fender heaves a sigh. "I'm going to let your attitude slide. But only because I've been in your shoes. And I've seen the rest of us standing right where you are. But take note, Squirrel, I don't fucking like it."

"Squirrel is right," Joker says. "We don't have to use the full weight of the Nightmare Room on Alan until we're sure. But if he is the one behind this, or he knows something, it's exactly what he deserves."

Fender glances around the room, takes in the expressions of every man. "Should we put it to another vote?"

Everyone nods.

"All those in favor of using the Nightmare Room for Alan, as a holding cell only until we know for sure his involvement?"

Two thumps all around the table.

"Thank you," I say, breathing a sigh of relief.

"Can I make a suggestion?"

Fender looks to Flash, as do I. "Go for it, brother."

"I think we should let Lexi talk to Alan first."

"No," I respond immediately. "Not happening."

"Hear me out, Squirrel," Flash insists. "She's trained to ask questions, the *right* questions. And Alan won't feel physically threatened by her. Maybe he'll open up more. If we go in there, he's going to be on the defensive straight out of the gate."

"He has a point," Riker says. "You trusted Lexi once and she came through. Not to mention we're thinking about making her the club's attorney. This'll give her a chance to really prove what she's got."

"And what if it is him behind all this?" I ask. "We're supposed to just put her in a room alone with him?"

"You'll be right outside, monitoring the entire thing," Fender says. "I will be too, for that matter. I wanna see what she has outside of a courtroom."

"I'll talk to her about it, but I'm not sure she'll agree."

"All you can do is try," Fender says, although the grin on his face says he expects me to make it happen.

"Yeah, okay."

The thing is, I know she'll agree. If she thinks it'll help me, help figure this shitstorm out, she'll agree. I just don't like it.

"Before we end church, I've got one more thing," Fender says and nods at Trainwreck. "Brother? Why don't you tell them?"

Trainwreck stands and faces me. "You'll be happy to know that your end of the deal with Judge Benton has been fulfilled."

## *Squirrel*

Shock settles over me. "What? How? It's only been a few days."

"Turns out I got pretty good at digging up information when I was researching the Church of Infinite Opportunity. Some might say I can now stand toe to toe with you in that regard," he teases.

"Keep dreaming," I scoff.

"Anyway, I spent the last few days pouring over all the police reports and interviews with potential witnesses. I had a few of the Michigan brothers make a few house calls." He grins. "The motel owner wasn't even on the police's radar as a suspect. A person of interest, yes, but he had an alibi, so he was scratched off the list."

"Would you just spit it out, Trainwreck," I bark.

"One of the witnesses, another guest of the motel, failed to mention that he'd seen the owner there that night. When Sling talked to this guest, he admitted what he saw. The owner went into the room with Maria and left two hours later, covered in blood."

"Why didn't he tell the cops this before?"

Trainwreck shrugs. "Don't know. Fear probably. But Sling got it out of him. Don't ask how... nasty story."

"I don't give a damn how he got the information, he got it. I take it Judge Benton has been informed?"

"I sent her everything I had earlier this morning. She was going to handle notifying the Sampsons. That part of all of this is over."

"That's great. It just seems..." I run my fingers through my hair, frustrated. "... stupid. It was something so simple, and because the cops were incompetent, or just didn't care about this particular victim because of her history, a murderer walked free for years. It's a waste."

"It is," Trainwreck agrees. "But if being a Soulless King has taught me anything, it's that evil comes in all forms. It's not just the people we take down. It's everywhere, in anyone."

"It's a hell of a thing, learning all of this the way we do," I say, feeling contemplative. "Before I prospected, I had no clue. I can't say it feels good to know what I know now."

"Brother," Fender says. "It never feels good to learn that there are two monsters for every one we take out. But we keep going because who else is going to do it? Certainly not the fucking cops," he snorts.

I nod before focusing on Trainwreck. "Thanks, brother. I appreciate your work on this."

"We're family, Squirrel. I've got your back, same way you have mine."

A lump forms in my throat, the last few weeks finally catching up to me. All I can do is nod again. He's right. We have one another's backs. Always have, always will.

And now I have Lexi's. I'll protect her, like I protect the Soulless Kings. And she'd do the same, even if it means being in the Nightmare Room and crossing lines she never dreamed of crossing.

How do I know this?

Because she's Lexi. She fights for what's right.

# Chapter Twenty-Four

*You can't get this wrong.*

**Lexi**

"I don't know if I can do this, Squirrel."

The monitor on the wall outside what he's called the Nightmare Room shows Alan leaning against the wall, arms crossed over his chest. I agreed to come here when Squirrel asked, but now that I'm here, I want to leave.

Squirrel runs his hands up and down my arms. "You can, Lexi. I'll be right here the whole time."

"Can't we just question him upstairs? At a table or something, like civilized human beings?"

"Civility went out the window when he brought you into this," Squirrel growls.

"We don't know it was him!" I cry, trying to get him to see reason.

Footsteps sound behind me, and I turn toward the staircase Squirrel led me down a few minutes ago. Fender walks toward us, his lips in a flat line.

"Is there a problem here?" he asks.

"No, no problem," Squirrel responds.

"Yes, there is," I argue. "This isn't right, Fender, and you know it."

"Lexi, listen up." Fender crosses his arms, his expression turning stern. "We brought you here because Squirrel believed in you. And because we believed your life was in danger. Do you really want to have to look over your shoulder for the rest of your life, wondering when the thing lurking in the shadows is going to leap on you? Or do you want to get in there..." He stabs a finger at the door. "... and ask a few questions so you can move on? Feel safe?"

"I want to feel safe."

"Then fucking show me that set of brass balls I know you have and get in there," he demands. "It's a meeting, just like you had with Squirrel in the jail. Nothing more, nothing less. It just looks different."

I look at the monitor again, really taking in what I see. Alan is an older man, probably in his mid-sixties. He's still leaning against the wall, his face displaying anger... and fear. What is he afraid of? What happens in this room that he's worried about?

And, more importantly, if he did nothing wrong, is not linked to this in any way, why is he scared?

Resolved to follow through with this, I look at Squirrel.

"You'll be here the entire time?"

"I promise." His eyes dart to Fender and back to mine. "We'll both be here."

I give a curt nod. "Open the door."

Fender opens a panel on the wall and presses a button.

## Squirrel

The door slides open, and immediately, Alan starts asking questions.

"Why am I here? What is going on?" He rushes the door, which is now sliding closed behind me. "Answer me, dammit!"

He pounds his fists on the steel, wearing himself out.

"Mr. Forney, please stop," I say quietly.

Surprisingly, he does. I don't turn around, but instead, stand there with my hands folded in front of me. An eerie calm washes over me, and it's... freeing somehow.

"All I want to do is ask you a few questions," I tell him.

He walks to the other side of the room and leans in the same spot he was in before. "Me first."

This guy is an attorney, just like me. I decide to give him a little grace. "Okay. Go ahead."

"Why am I here?"

"That wasn't explained to you?" I ask.

He narrows his eyes at me, much like I'd do if a witness was beating around the bush instead of answering my question.

"Of course not," he blusters.

"I'm sorry about that. From what I can gather, the Soulless Kings just want information."

"And they sent you? Why not just ask me themselves?"

I shrug. "I don't know. But this is the situation we both find ourselves in, so please, let's just be professional about it."

"Little girl, you don't know these people like I do. This room isn't used for just anything. It's a torture chamber." I keep my face impassive even though bile rises up the back of my throat. "If I'm in here, they've already convicted me of whatever the hell they think I did."

"No, that's not true," I assure him, even though I don't

think he's entirely wrong. I tilt my head. "But it does beg the question, what do they think you did?"

"I don't know," he cries, throwing up his hands. He doesn't avert his gaze, nor does he show any signs of deception, that I'm aware of. Either he's really good, or he's telling me the truth and he has no clue.

*You can't get this wrong, Lexi, so you better be sure before you walk out of this place.*

"Why were you so upset when the Soulless Kings hired me to defend Squirrel?"

"Are you kidding me?" he counters. "You're a newbie attorney who had never defended a murder suspect before. Not to mention, I've got way more knowledge of the club than you do. I wanted him to beat the charge, not get shipped off never to be seen again."

"Fair enough," I concede. I can't say that I wouldn't have been upset in his shoes. But the fact remains that it doesn't prove he's not responsible for all of it in the first place. "Next question. Once they hired me, why did you remain so resistant? You know how the club works, why continue to fight what they wanted?"

"Because it's my job. As a lawyer, we sometimes have to fight for what's right for our clients, even if they can't see what that is at the time."

*True.*

"I can admire that," I tell him, surprised at how much he seems to align with my way of thinking. "I'm the same way."

"Then you get it."

"Sort of. What I don't get is why you still chose to not show up until right before the trial. We had work to do, and you weren't there. Where were you?"

"Believe it or not, I have a life outside of what I do for this club. I had family business to take care of."

## *Squirrel*

"Like what?"

"I really don't think that's any of your—"

"Mr. Forney, I'll remind you where we are." I push my glasses up my nose, annoyed with how they keep slipping. "The Soulless Kings have obviously made it my business to find out the answers to every question I'm asking. I suggest you answer." I glance over my shoulder at the door and then back to him. "Or maybe you'd rather talk to Squirrel or Fender? I can arrange that."

"No, no," he insists, frantically waving his hands in front of him. "That won't be necessary. They're more apt to punish me for perceived wrongs and ask questions later."

"Okay then, answer me. What family business were you taking care of?"

Alan heaves a sigh and his face falls. For the first time since walking into this room, I sense a sadness coming from him. He drops his head for a moment before squaring his shoulders and lifting his eyes to mine. There's a sheen to them I wish I wasn't seeing.

"My wife was recently diagnosed with breast cancer, and her treatments happened to coincide with when you wanted me in Michigan. I couldn't miss her first one."

Sympathy pours out of me for the man. He seems genuinely upset, almost as if his world is falling apart. But sadness can be faked.

*It can, but is he faking?*

"I'm sorry to hear that." If he's telling the truth, then he's not the enemy. And I'm not a cold-hearted bitch. "I didn't know."

"Of course not. I didn't tell anyone."

"Why not? Maybe if you had, we wouldn't be here."

Alan pushes off the wall and takes a few steps toward

me. "Miss Cantor, do you tell all your clients your personal business?"

"No, I suppose I don't."

"I didn't want the club to think I was incapable of putting my personal stuff aside in order to effectively do my job."

"But that's exactly what happened. You proved that you can't do that."

"They had you." His eyes plead with me. "Fender made it clear, as did Squirrel, that you were the attorney of record. At that point, yes, you're right, I put my wife first."

*As he should have.*

I believe him. I believe that he's innocent and that whoever the real threat is, used him as a scapegoat, something to divert our attention.

"Excuse me a moment."

I turn toward the door and nod, exactly how Squirrel told me to if I wanted out. When it slides open, I rush through, as if escaping something vile. The thing is, it didn't feel vile. Alan didn't seem vile to me.

Squirrel takes one look at me and says, "You believe him, don't you?"

"You don't?"

"I don't know what to believe," he says.

Fender paces the hallway. "Squirrel, dig up the wife's medical records, see what you can find. If he's telling the truth, we'll let him go. He's still fired, but he won't be harmed."

"And while we wait on Squirrel to do that?" I ask, thinking of the man still in the Nightmare Room.

"Already done," Squirrel says, holding up his cell. "He's telling the truth."

"Dammit," Fender says.

## *Squirrel*

"At least you know he didn't betray you," I say, trying to focus on the bright side of this. I chew on my bottom lip. "Poor guy. He was just being a good husband, and look where it got him."

"He made his choices. He could have said something at any point," Squirrel points out. His shoulders relax. "But you're right. He's not a bad guy. Just an idiot."

"Let him go," Fender says before walking up the stairs and disappearing.

"Why do I feel like I made things worse?" I ask Squirrel.

"You didn't Lexi. You got the truth out of him."

I nod. "But we're back at square one now, aren't we?"

"Yeah, yeah we are."

# Chapter Twenty-Five

*What if...?*

**Squirrel**

Lexi is sprawled next to me in bed, her leg thrown over mine and her arm across my chest. She hasn't slept in her own room in the week since she questioned Alan in the Nightmare Room. I don't know why that seems to have been a turning point, but who am I to question it?

She tightens her arm around me. "What are you thinking about?"

I hug her close. "How much I like waking up next to you."

Lexi shifts until she's straddling me. She moves her hips, feeding my morning erection. "Is that all you like?"

I grip her sides and lift her so I can line up with her slick pussy. I push my way in, reveling in the way her body fits mine.

From the moment I met her, I knew she wasn't what she

seemed. She's proven that, over and over again, but never more so than in the bedroom. A button-down, strait-laced woman she is not.

Lexi lifts her arms above her head, like a sleek cat stretching, and her tits beg to be touched. I squeeze them, tweak her nipples, before sitting up and sucking the pink beauties into my mouth.

Her moans fill the room, long little mewls that fuel the fire in my cock. I let go of her nipples with a pop and flip her over onto her back. I want to let her have control, but I can't. Not now.

I'm too far gone. Doesn't take much where Lexi is concerned.

"Fuck me, Squirrel."

I grab her hands and wrap her fingers around the spindles that make up the headboard. "Hang on, baby."

And then I take it slow, doing the exact opposite of what her body is begging for. She tries to buck her hips, force me to go faster, but I don't. I want to drag this out as long as I can.

I lean over her and press my lips to her ear. "Feel my cock inside of you. Feel it stretching your wet pussy, claiming it. Close your eyes and just feel."

Lifting my head, a lazy smile tugs my lips when I see her closed lids.

"That's my girl."

My strokes remain slow, controlled, but with purpose. It's much different than our first time together, but just as incredible. I reach between our bodies and press my thumb to her clit, while continuing to glide in and out of her. Within seconds, her walls tighten, spasm around my cock and demand a release from me.

I oblige. I don't increase my speed, wanting to drag out

the pleasure. I lay my body over hers, maintaining the rhythm with my hips and hold her while we both take what we need from each other.

When my orgasm is over, I roll to the side, pulling her with me. Her head is tucked into the crook of my shoulder and her leg returns to its place over mine.

"That never gets old," she says.

"Certainly not in the last week." I chuckle. I brush my fingertips over her arm. "And probably not ever."

We lay there in silence, neither one wanting to ruin the moment, until Bug barks, forcing us to face the day.

"I'll go take him out," I tell her. "Why don't you hop in the shower? I'll join you in a few."

"Sounds good."

I hop out of bed and race to take Bug out to do his business, a shower with Lexi at the forefront of my mind. We may have just gone a round, but I'm always up for more. When I return inside, I'm surprised not to hear the shower running already. I thought for sure she'd be in there, all soapy and ready.

I hang Bug's leash by the door and make my way back down the hall to the bedroom. Bug stays on my heels, as he likes to do, and when we enter the room, he races past me to jump on the bed next to Lexi.

She's holding her cell phone in her hand, and she's staring at it like it's grown a head.

"What's wrong?"

Lexi lifts her eyes to mine, and I see the tears just as they spill over her lashes. Bug tries to lick her face, to console her in only the way dogs can, but it doesn't slow the torrent. I rush to the bed and lift her phone from her hands so I can see what's upsetting her so much.

*Squirrel*

**You could have put a stop to this.**

"Was I wrong?" Lexi asks through her sniffles. "About Alan? Was I wrong?"

"No," I tell her, not sure if I'm lying or not.

If she was wrong, so was I. I checked out his story, but what if...?

I pull Lexi onto my lap and hold her while she cries. I tell her that it'll be okay, that she wasn't wrong, all the while praying I'm not lying.

*You're lying.*

"I believed him."

"So did I, Lexi. So did I."

She pushes away from me and takes her glasses off to clean them on the sheet. "Maybe this is exactly what it was before. Whoever is really doing this is trying to point fingers."

"Maybe."

"You don't believe that do you?" she asks.

"I don't know what to believe anymore."

Lexi takes a deep breath. "Call the guys and let them know."

I want to stay with her, take care of her, reassure her. But she's right. I have to let my brothers know.

"I'll just be in the kitchen, okay? I'm going to call Fender."

Lexi nods, but it's stiff. She hugs Bug close to her, as if he's her lifeline while I'll be gone. I make my way to the kitchen and take my phone off my charger. Things have been quiet, so I've been leaving it out there. Besides, if they really need me, they know where I live.

"Yo," Fender answers on the third ring.

"We may have been wrong about Alan," I spit out.

"Squirrel, you checked everything out. Where is this coming from?"

"Lexi got another text this morning." I repeat what the bastard sent to her.

"It's probably the same person trying to throw us off again."

"And if it's not?" I counter, my gut telling me there's more to it than that.

"Squirrel, you need to just spit it out. What is it you want me to do? We've already got everyone trying to figure this one out. We've got feelers out everywhere. You know as well as I do this isn't going to be figured out like we're used to. Other than a few texts, this guy isn't doing anything."

"Bring Alan in," I demand. "Let me have a crack at him."

"We have to put that to a vote, especially since we already let him go once."

"Then call church," I bark.

Fender's intake of breath comes through the line, and I know I'm going to pay for that. Oh well.

"I'll call church, but this is the last time we're bringing him in. Got it?"

"Got it."

"Jesus, bro. If you're wrong, *again*, we're screwing with a man who's just trying to take care of his sick wife. You get that, right? How would you feel in his shoes if it was Lexi with breast cancer?"

I take a deep breath and try to hear what he's saying. He's making a point, no doubt a very good one, but it's not sinking in. Not like he wants.

"Just call church. I'll be there in ten."

I disconnect the call and toss the cell on the counter.

## Squirrel

Either Fender's getting soft, or he really doesn't trust my judgment.

*Should he trust it? Especially when you don't even know if you do?*

My muscles coil with frustration, and I pound the counter with my fists. The pain ricochets through my arms, and I welcome it because it's real. I know it's real. I don't question the pain, because I feel it.

Footsteps sound behind me, and I turn in time to see Lexi and Bug walk into the kitchen.

"Judging by the look on your face, that call didn't go like you wanted."

"Fender's calling church, so there's that." I thrust a hand through my hair. "I'm gonna have to go to the clubhouse. Why don't you come with me?"

She shakes her head. "No, go. I'm going to stay here and make some calls. I haven't talked to my parents at all since we left Michigan, and I should probably do that. What better time than now?"

"Are you sure?"

"Squirrel, go. We both have things to do. I'll see you when you get home, okay?"

"Okay. If I see the girls, I'll send them over. Maybe they can keep you company."

Lexi isn't stupid. She has to know what I'm doing. I don't want to leave her alone.

She nods, accepting that I'm not going to change my mind.

"That would be nice."

Satisfied with that, I kiss her on the cheek and walk toward the front door.

"Ah, Squirrel?"

I look over my shoulder at her. "Yeah?"

She scans my body and grins with appreciation. Her smirk is big when she looks back at my face. "Might want to put some actual clothes on first."

I glance down and remember I'd only thrown boxer briefs on to take Bug out.

"Motherfucker."

# Chapter Twenty-Six

*You have this place. You have Squirrel.*

**Lexi**

After ushering Squirrel out the door, I decide to make myself some breakfast. I worked up an appetite earlier. It takes mere minutes to whip up some scrambled eggs, and when I realize I made too much, I share them with Bug.

"I kinda like it here, Bug," I tell the boxer. "How about you?" His head tilts, but that's about all the answer I'm going to get.

It takes about as long to clean up as it did to make the eggs. Once that's done, I take a shower. I know I'm procrastinating, but I really don't want to call my parents. I just know I have to. They at least deserve to know where their daughter is.

When I know I can't put it off any longer, I return to the bedroom and sit on the bed. I dial their number and wait.

"Hello."

"Hi Mom."

"I was wondering when you'd call," she says, no hesitation, no excitement that it's her daughter.

"Did you get the money I sent?"

"Yes, a few weeks ago." Mom sighs. "I have to say, it was more than I was expecting."

"I should hope so. Five thousand dollars is a little more than what you were used to."

"It is," she admits. "But it leaves me wondering… how did you get the money?"

I roll my eyes. "Work, mom. I told you, I was starting fresh. I'm doing really well, thanks for asking."

I can't keep the annoyance from my tone, and honestly, I don't even care to. If Squirrel has taught me anything, it's that I deserve better. I'm enough, whether my parents think so or not.

"So you'll be able to send more soon?"

My control snaps. "Is that all that matters to you? Money?"

"We could really use it," she persists. "And if you're doing so well…"

Guilt swells. She's right. I'm well off financially now. And will continue to be that way if I stay and work full time for the club.

*You're going to stay.*

But I want my parents to love me, to care about me for more than what I can provide them. Is that so much to ask?

"I moved to Oregon," I blurt out.

"You did what?"

"I moved to Oregon," I repeat, past sugarcoating anything, past pretending like any conversation with this woman is normal. "I will continue to send you and Dad

*Squirrel*

money, just as I have been. But I won't be calling again after today. I can't keep doing this with you, Mom."

"Doing what?"

"This," I cry. "Calling you and hoping for a different reaction when you realize it's me when you answer the phone. I can't keep pretending that we're normal, that I have great parents who are proud of me. Maybe you were at one point, but now? I'm not so sure."

"You chose this, Lexi, remember that."

"Yeah, Mom." I nod even though she can't see me. "Yeah, I guess I did. Tell Dad I love him. And I love you too."

"Lexi, this is—"

I disconnect the call, not interested in hearing any more of what she has to say. Tears flow down my cheeks at having severed my last tie to anything. I have no one anymore. No home, no anchor.

*You have this place. You have Squirrel.*

As hard as it is to accept, that phone call solidifies my decision to stay. I care about Squirrel, and if it doesn't work out, Oregon is a big place. I can start over if I have to.

*You won't have to.*

A knock on the door startles me. Bug races from the room, barking as the knocking gets louder, more persistent. I set my phone on the nightstand and make my way to see who it is.

"I'm coming," I call out, annoyed at whoever is getting my dog all worked up.

I yank open the door and see Charlie standing there, with Holland and Sylvia behind her.

"Squirrel sent you," I accuse, secretly glad to see them.

In the short time I've been here, I've only met them on a

few occasions but know they're exactly what I need at a time like this: friends.

"He did," Charlie confirms. "But we've been meaning to come over anyway." She squints and stares at my face. "Hey, why have you been crying?"

Charlie pushes past me into the house, and the other two women follow.

"What did the bastard do?" Holland asks. "You can tell us."

"Men are idiots," Sylvia says. "I mean, Trainwreck isn't, but the rest are."

"Says the girl who recently got engaged," Charlie teases, rolling her eyes.

Yep, they're exactly what I need.

"Squirrel didn't do anything," I tell them. "Can I get you anything to drink?"

"I'd love some coffee," Charlie says. "As much as liquor sounds better, I've gotta work at the shop later and Fender will have my ass if I fuck up a bike."

"Same for me," Holland says.

"Me three."

"You got it."

I put on another pot to brew, and while I wait, I fill a plate with cookies that I had Squirrel get at the store for me.

*What the hell are you doing?*

It hits me then. I have no clue how to act with friends. I've spent most of my life focused on school and family. Sure, I had a few friends through grade school, but I still cared more about pleasing my parents than fostering those friendships. And then there was college, law school, work. There was always something more important.

"You don't need to wait on us, ya know?"

## Squirrel

I whirl around and see Holland standing in the doorway. "I wasn't... I..." I shrug.

"I get it." She pushes off the wall and walks toward me. After wrapping her arm around my shoulder, she says, "We're all friends here, okay?"

I nod.

"Now," she nods toward the coffee pot. "Help me get the mugs filled, and we'll go chill."

I laugh, finally feeling a little at ease. "Sounds good."

"So, why were you crying before you answered the door?" Charlie asks after taking a sip of her coffee.

And just like that, I find myself telling them everything about my parents, about how I'm fed up and not going to put up with it anymore. It feels good to unburden it all.

"Good for you," Sylvia says. "Trust me, if anyone knows about shitty family, it's Charlie and I. Someday when we have more time, we'll tell you all about it."

I glance at my watch. How has two hours passed already?

"Shit, I guess you probably should go. Work and all that?"

"Before you know it, you'll settle in and have a routine." Charlie stands and hands me her empty mug. "You're coming to the clubhouse tonight, right?"

"I don't know. Squirrel didn't mention it."

"Girl, you don't need an invite from him to come. We'll see you there around nine, okay?"

"Oh, well okay then. I'll be there."

"And wear something... sexy."

After the three of them leave, I clean up the kitchen and think about what to wear tonight. An image of a certain outfit Squirrel made sure I had enters my mind, and I make my way to my closet to make sure it's in there and not packed in a box over in the clubhouse basement.

Just as I locate it, Bug goes crazy, and I hear a knock on the door again. Thinking one of the girls forgot to tell me something, I race to answer it.

When I pull open the door again, my stomach bottoms out.

Alan Forney is standing there, a gun at his side. Bug continues to bark, but it's no longer out of warning. He's seen Alan before, so he doesn't see him as a threat. He's just excited to see a familiar face.

Alan lifts the gun and points it at Bug.

"Shut him up before I have to."

# Chapter Twenty-Seven

*I don't like to hurt people, but like I told Lexi, I will if I have to.*

### Squirrel

"It's Lexi. Leave a message at the beep."

"It's me. I've gotta run with the guys to do a few things and wanted to let you know I'd be a little later than I thought. You're probably on the phone with your parents. I hope that's going well."

I hesitate before ending the call, three more words on the tip of my tongue. In the end, I don't say them and disconnect.

"Jesus, it's like that already?" Joker taunts as he slaps my back.

"Like what?"

"You're fuckin' whipped, bro," he says. "You called to tell her what you're doing and that you'll be late. It's like *that*."

"Shut the fuck up."

Joker shrugs. "You can fight it all you want, but when

you're making a phone call like that, you're so far gone you're gonna need more than a bus ticket to get back."

"Leave him alone," Fender says as he strides past us. "I need him focused, and if you get him all up in his head about feelings and shit, he won't be focused."

"I'm focused, Prez."

"Better be."

Church ended just before I called Lexi, with a vote to find Alan and bring him back to the clubhouse so I could have a go at him in the Nightmare Room. We're all going, since we don't know exactly where he'll be. I, along with Riker, Piston, and Greaser will go to his house while Fender, Joker, Gibson and Flash will go to his office.

"Let's ride," Fender shouts.

The sound of rumbling Harley's fills my ears, and a calm washes over me that I haven't felt since the moment I slipped from Lexi's body this morning. And it can only get better from here.

An hour later, I second guess myself. Alan isn't at his house, and according to the text from Joker, he's not at his office either. Fender makes the call to return to the clubhouse and reconvene to see if we can track Alan another way.

On the ride back, my mind wanders to Lexi. I wonder what she's doing. How did the call go with her parents? Is she hanging out with Charlie and the others? Is she having fun?

Will she stay when this is all over?

So many questions roll through my mind, all without answers.

The answers remain elusive, even as I drive past Burly at the main property gate and weave through the long drive to park in front of the clubhouse.

## *Squirrel*

"We'll find him," Greaser says as he passes me and walks up the steps.

"Hell, he's probably not our guy anyway," Joker comments. "I mean, I'm on board with you questioning him again because something isn't right, but do you really think he's got the clout to manage what he had to manage to get you arrested?"

"I don't know," I admit. "That's the problem."

"Well, let's go see what else we can dig up."

Joker takes the steps two at a time, and I follow him inside. Fender is at the bar talking to Margo, while Royal sits at the other end sipping a drink. The others are mingling, no doubt waiting to go back to the drawing board to figure out how to find Alan.

"Yo, Royal, how was your post today?" I ask, taking the stool next to him. "Weren't you on duty when we left?"

"I was," Royal confirms. "Nice of you to stop and chat on your way out."

There's humor in his tone, and I chuckle. "Yeah, sorry 'bout that. We were on a mission."

Typically, whenever I go through the gate, I'll stop and talk to whoever is on duty. I've been at that post too many times to count, and usually, it's boring as hell. Today, my head was elsewhere.

"I figured as much."

"When's your next shift?" I ask.

"Same time tomorrow." He takes the last sip of his beer before shoving off his stool. "Which is why I'm going to go smoke a joint and then take a nap. If we party tonight, I won't get shit for sleep."

"Sounds good, brother. If I don't see you later, I'll make sure to stop by and break up some of the boredom tomorrow."

"Bring your girl too." He laughs, starting to walk away. "Break up some of the shitty scenery."

I shake my head at the prospect. He can be an ass sometimes, but he's a good kid.

"Oh, I almost forgot," Royal says, turning back to face me.

"What?"

"Alan Forney came by. Said he wanted to give Lexi everything he had pertaining to the club since she was taking over for him. Had a shit ton of boxes in his car so I sent him to your place."

My blood runs cold.

"What did you just say?" I seethe.

"What?" Royal asks, glancing from one brother to the next. "I sent him to your place."

"When?"

"About a half hour ago. Right before my shift ended."

I take off at a run, certain that nothing good awaits me at my place.

"Squirrel, where are you going?" Fender yells as I barrel through the front door.

I don't stop to answer him. He's either going to follow or not. Either way, I've got to get to Lexi because there's no good reason for Alan to be at my place. His whole story about needing to transfer files is bullshit. There are no files. At least paper copies. Everything Alan ever needs is electronic.

I should know... I built the system they're stored on, the same system he has to log into to gain access to them. Lexi would have had all that info at her fingertips as soon as she had a password.

The ride to my house seems to take hours, but it's only minutes. Precious minutes Lexi might not have.

## Squirrel

*You're overreacting, dude. You don't know that Alan is behind this.*

Yeah, I do. He's behind it as sure as Lexi makes my dick hard.

I know it.

Alan's fancy Mercedes is parked in front of my house, the one the club paid for. I throw my leg over the bike and bend to grab the gun in my boot.

I don't like to hurt people, but like I told Lexi, I will if I have to.

# Chapter Twenty-Eight

*This is how I die. Beaten and burned.*

**Lexi**

*Thirty minutes earlier...*

"Shut him up before I have to."

"Alan, what are you doing?"

Bug continues to bark.

"I'm not messing around, Lexi. Shut him up."

"He's a dog, Alan. They bark." I'm not trying to upset Alan, but I'm not exactly sure how I'm supposed to shut a dog up, at least not for long. "I can give him a toy, and that'll keep him quiet for a while."

"Fine. Do that, and then put him in the basement." He waves the gun at me. "But no funny business."

I walk to the other side of the living room where Squirrel put Bug's basket of toys, making sure to keep my hands visible. "Come pick a toy, Bug," I call to my dog, trying to keep things as normal for Bug as possible. He's a sweet dog, and I don't want that to get him hurt.

## Squirrel

"Just give him one!" Alan shouts, kicking the door shut as he steps completely inside, the gun still pointed in our direction.

I grab a stuffed animal that Bug likes to gnaw on when he's tired. Rather than give it to him, I lead him to the basement door with it. Once I open the door, I toss it down, praying Bug will go after it. Fortunately, he does.

*Thank you, Squirrel for insisting we get him used to steps.*

After closing the door to ensure Bug stays put, I turn around to face Alan. His face is sweaty and red, although from rage or stress, I'm not sure. Nor am I sure which I'd prefer. Both make a person unpredictable, and Alan is already that.

"Alan, we can talk about this," I say. "You haven't done anything yet, so this can stop, right here, right now."

Alan throws his head back and laughs, although the sound is devoid of humor. "I like your optimism, Lexi. But it's lost on me."

"No, Alan, it's not. Think about your wife. In her condition, do you really want to put her through whatever the consequences of this will be?"

He smirks. "You bought that story?" He shakes his head. "Of course you did. You wouldn't be able to spot a lie if it ran up and bit you on that tight little ass of yours."

I shudder at the thought of him staring at *any* part of my body. Confusion manages to sift through the disgust. Squirrel found the medical records. I saw them with my own eyes.

"Lexi, Lexi, Lexi," he sing-songs. "Squirrel isn't the only one with his particular set of skills."

Realization hits me. "You faked the records? But how?"

He shrugs. "Money talks. And I've made a lot of it

working for the Soulless Kings." Alan tsks. "I'm disappointed, Lexi. One of the first things I learned after becoming their attorney was that everyone has a price. Lawyers, judges, cops, doctors... hospital administrators. It wasn't that hard to convince someone to create a false record."

"But why?" I cry.

"Like I told you before, the club took something from me, and Squirrel made it possible."

This isn't new information to me, and I fear I won't get anything new before he loses it and puts a bullet in my head.

"It's a funny thing when a man learns his entire life was a lie."

"I'm not following."

"Then listen harder!" he shouts, spittle flying from his mouth.

Alan lunges at me. I try to escape him, but he's deceptively strong for an older man. He grabs my hands and yanks them behind my back. Then he takes a zip tie out of his pocket and secures my wrists together.

"You're coming with me."

"Where are we going?" I ask as he drags me toward the back door.

"Somewhere a little more private."

He pulls me through the door, out into the afternoon air. I may not be equipped to fight back physically, but I've got a set of lungs that may help.

I scream, as loud and as long as I can. I don't know if anyone will hear me at the clubhouse, or anywhere else on the property for that matter, but I have to try.

Unfortunately, my action doesn't go unpunished. Pain explodes in my cheek when Alan hits me with the butt of

## Squirrel

the gun, and I fall to the ground. My hip bounces off a tree root, and tears spring to my eyes.

"Get up," Alan demands.

I roll to my back and try to sit up, but my head spins, and I collapse. More pain radiates through my ribs as Alan kicks me.

"I said get up!"

"I'm trying," I cry.

Alan reaches down and grabs my bicep to haul me to my feet. I sway but somehow manage to stay upright. He starts to drag me again, into the trees. We don't walk far, maybe two hundred yards, before he comes to an abrupt stop and shoves me against a tree trunk.

"This is good enough."

I dart my head around, looking for anything I could maybe use as a weapon. I know it's useless. Even if I found something, my hands are bound.

"What are you going to do?"

Alan grins, and for a moment, it's like I'm looking at the Joker. He's crazy.

"I told you Squirrel made it possible for the Soulless Kings to take from me." I slowly nod. "I'm returning the favor."

Without warning, he delivers a right jab to my jaw, and blood spurts from my mouth. Dots float around my head as I fight to maintain consciousness.

"I was adopted, did you know that?"

Another punch.

"I had a brother."

Alan grabs me by the hair and pulls my head toward him. He's so close I can smell his breath. He's been drinking, that much is clear, and bile rises up the back of my throat at the stench.

"Of course, I didn't know that until it was too late."

"Wh-what are you talking about?"

Alan shoves my head into the tree trunk, and bark digs into my scalp. "You don't get to ask any more questions."

This guy is insane. How do you reason with that?

*You don't.*

"Wanna know what I found when I went looking for my biological family?"

I say nothing.

"No?" He tilts his head. "Too bad. I'm going to tell you anyway." Alan shoves me to the ground, and I land on my knees. "It wasn't a closed adoption, so no red tape. When I was ready, I started looking. It wasn't hard. I got their names." Alan squats and puts the gun to my chin. "But I held onto them. It's a process, ya know? First, get the names. Then wait for the guts to actually use that information to meet them."

Alan taps the gun against my temple, almost as if he's telling me to think about it. Oh, I'm thinking. But not about what he's telling me. I don't give a shit about what he's telling me.

I'm thinking about Squirrel. I'm thinking about waking up next to him in the mornings. About trying to survive this so I can see him again. I'm thinking about grabbing life by the horns and not letting another day go by without telling Squirrel how I feel, socially acceptable time frames be damned.

Alan stands and walks behind me. I try to turn my head to see where he's going, but I can't. Everything hurts too bad. I don't even hesitate. I try to get to my feet, hope flaring that maybe, just maybe, I can get away.

It's short-lived though. Alan reappears, and when he sees me struggling, he laughs.

## Squirrel

"Where do you think you're going?"

I turn my head toward him. My eyes are swelling, making it difficult to see much, but there's no mistaking what he's holding. The gun remains, but he's gripping a bright red gas can in his other hand.

*That's it. This is how I die. Beaten and burned.*

I crumble to the ground in a heap of bruises and blood. I don't want to die, but I don't have it in me to fight.

*Squirrel, please, help.*

"As I was saying," Alan begins. "When I finally was ready to reach out and meet my biological family, do you know what I found?"

I shake my head, or at least I think I do.

"A whole lot of nothing!"

Alan starts pouring gas around my body. The distinct scent wafts up my nostrils, and this time, when the bile rises, I don't hold back. I vomit, my body heaving, shaking. The combination of puke and gas does nothing to calm my stomach, and I continue until there's nothing left.

"Lexi!"

I try to lift my head at the sound of my name, but the feel of grass, sticks and dirt doesn't go away.

"Lexi, where are you?"

Alan squats again, but I can barely make him out through the slits my eyes have become.

"Seems we have company."

His face disappears, but his voice doesn't. It becomes distant, like he stood up and turned away from me.

"I wasn't planning on making him watch, but I can adapt."

# Chapter Twenty-Nine

*Don't you dare die on me.*

### Squirrel

"Lexi!"

I search the main level of the house and don't find her. I stand in the living room and survey the space. Nothing seems out of place, there's no sign of a struggle. But she's not here, and neither is Alan.

Bug's insistent barking pulls my attention toward the basement, and I rush to the door and yank it open. Bug tears past me, keeping his nose to the ground. He goes straight for the back door and jumps up on the glass.

"Where is she, Bug?" I ask, sliding open the door.

He races out and makes his way toward the woods. When he reaches the edge, he barks fiercely, hopping around while he waits for me to catch up. When I do, I point a finger at him.

"Sit." He obeys. "Stay."

## Squirrel

I don't bother waiting to see if he listens. He will. Lexi has trained him well.

"Lexi!" I call out.

No response. I keep running, and within seconds, a smell tickles my nostrils. I follow the distinct smell of gas.

"Lexi, where are you?"

A few minutes pass before I get a response.

"Keep coming, Squirrel. You're not far."

Alan.

"If you hurt her, I won't wait for the Nightmare Room to kill you," I call to him.

I keep running, and when they come into view, I stop in my tracks.

Alan is standing over Lexi, who's on the ground in a bloody heap. My stomach bottoms out, but I remain where I am. I don't want to set him off. The smell of gas is much stronger, and based on the wet dirt around her, she's surrounded by it.

"She better be alive," I seethe, lifting my gun.

"She is... for now." He points his gun at Lexi's head. "Tit for tat, Squirrel. You pull your trigger, I pull mine. You know I'll get a shot off before I drop. The Soulless Kings taught me well, after all."

"What do you want?"

"It's simple, really. Revenge." Alan reaches into his pocket and pulls out a Zippo lighter. "It's a concept I believe you're very familiar with."

"Revenge for what?"

Alan shakes his head. "How many times do I have to tell you? You took something from me."

"What?"

I'm talking to Alan, but my attention is divided between

him and Lexi. I need to see a sign of life. Movement, a moan, anything. I don't trust a word he says.

"My family."

"Sq..."

"Lexi?"

"I told you," Alan rages. "She's alive."

Alan walks toward me, stopping halfway between where Lexi lies, and I stand.

"In the interest of time, I'll give you the quick version of why I'm here," Alan says matter-of-factly. "I was adopted, tracked down the names of my birth family, and years later, wanted to meet them."

"What does this have to do with me or the club?" I nod toward Lexi. "Or her?"

"I'm getting to that." He narrows his eyes. "Does the name Jack Ross mean anything to you?"

I search my brain for the name and come up empty. It feels reminiscent of when I was asked about Maria Sampson. Two names. No recognition. The only difference is that the police weren't threatening the love of my life's existence. Alan is.

*Why?*

"I can see that didn't ring any bells," he says, pulling me back to the present. "Let me refresh your memory. Jack Ross, fifty-six, a dealer for the club. Ended up taking off with a lot of Soulless Kings' money, left them holding the bag with their supplier."

I'm starting to put the pieces together.

"And he was your biological..."

"Brother, you moron," Alan sneers. "He was my biological brother. Who I never got to meet because you tracked him down so the club could kill him."

## Squirrel

*That's what this is about? He tried to get me for murder because of this?*

"Plan A was to have you convicted of murder and then taken out in prison. That way, my hands were clean." He glances over her shoulder at Lexi. "But then she got in the way of that. So, here we are." Alan shrugs. "Plan B. Two birds, one stone." He walks backward toward Lexi, keeping his eyes on me. "I kill her, take her away from you before you even really have a chance to get started."

"You do that, I kill you."

"I know. And I've made peace with that. But I'll die knowing you will spend the rest of your life wondering what could have been, just like me."

"What about your wife?" I ask, willing to try anything.

"She's a cold-hearted bitch that married me for my money. She'll be thrilled when I die."

Alan lifts the Zippo to his side so it's directly above Lexi. He flips the top open and the smile that spreads across his lips will be a sight that will remain in my memory forever.

My eyes drop to the ground, and I see he's standing in the gas. He never meant to walk away from this. He knows if he drops the lighter, he'll go up in flames right along with Lexi.

"Alan, don't do this, man," I plead.

He rolls his finger over the wheel, striking the flint inside, and flame dances above the chrome. My hand tightens on my gun. I want to pull the trigger, but if I do, Lexi still dies.

"All I ask is that you bury my body wherever you buried my brother's. Maybe I can get to know him in death."

Alan turns his weapon on himself so fast, I don't even have time to react.

Bang!

"No!"

Alan drops, taking the Zippo with him. I lunge forward, the heat of the flames engulfing the two of them threatening to swallow me up. Ignoring the pain, I grab Lexi's arm and drag her away from the fire, away from certain death. After taking off my shirt, I slap it on her arms and legs, where the fire still burns, until it's out.

The scent of burning flesh and smoke threatens to double me over, but I lift her in my arms and carry her to the edge of the woods, where surprisingly, Bug is still sitting.

He rushes forward when I set his person on the grass and licks her face. I check Lexi's pulse and don't find one.

"Don't die on me, Lexi," I beg, starting CPR. "Don't you dare die on me."

# Chapter Thirty

*Only Squirrel. Always Squirrel.*

**Lexi**

Don't you dare die on me.
 Don't you dare die on me.
 Don't you dare die on me.
Beeping machines and the shuffle of feet mingle with Squirrel's words. I don't know how long I've been in the hospital, but I've held onto any sound and those words as hard as I can. Almost as if by doing that, I'll somehow stay closer to life and further away from death.

"Lexi, baby, I'm here."

Squirrel.

I try to smile, but I don't think he can see it around the tube down my throat. The contraption is annoying, but it's why I can breathe, so I'm glad it's there.

"Alan's dead."

He's told me this already, several times. But maybe he's the one who needs to keep hearing it to believe it's true.

"I'm so sorry this happened, that I wasn't there."

Squirrel has also apologized, over and over again. I don't know how he could possibly blame himself. Alan was a man with demons bigger than we could imagine. Besides, I'm the one who should be apologizing. I'm the one who believed Alan's lies in the first place.

And I will apologize. As soon as I wake up.

I reach out for Squirrel's hand and squeeze. Only I don't feel his skin against mine. I don't feel him at all.

I want to feel Squirrel. Let me feel Squirrel!

Beep. Beep. Beep.

Why are the machines going crazy? What's happening?

I can feel my heart race, pound until it feels like it's going to break open my chest and thump right out of my body.

"Out of the way!"

Okay, that's my nurse's voice.

*Someone please tell me what is going on.*

A cold sensation runs through my veins, and the beeping slows. So does my heartbeat. The quiet is nice, but now the sounds in the room sound far away.

No, don't go. I need to hear you. Squirrel?

*Don't you dare die on me.*
*Don't you dare die on me.*
*Don't you dare die on me.*

I focus on those six words. I don't know how long I focus on them, but I know I can't stop. If I stop, I die.

*Don't you dare die on me.*
*Don't you dare—*

"C'mon, Balls. You need to wake up. Squirrel's losing his mind."

Sling? What the hell is he doing here? Wait, they didn't ship me back to Michigan did they?

## Squirrel

*Don't you dare die on me.*

"Hey, Lexi, it's Steph."

"And Courtney."

"We just wanted you to know we're here. And we're not going home until you wake up."

Good. Not in Michigan.

"Girl, the brothers back in Michigan are seriously missing my bartending skills, so what do ya say? Wake up so we can go back to them?"

*Don't you dare die on me.*
*Don't you dare die on me.*

"Lexi. It's been two weeks. I'm drowning here without you."

Squirrel's back!

Wait, did he say two weeks? No. No, that can't be right.

"I had the guys move all your stuff into my house. I know we talked about finding you a place of your own. But baby, I can't let you go." Sigh. "At least wake up so we can argue about where you're going to live."

*Don't you dare die on me.*
*Don't you dare die on me.*
*Don't you dare die on me.*

"Miss Cantor's condition is improving, believe it or not." My doctor is speaking, but to who?

"How do ya figure, doc?" Squirrel sounds frustrated. And tired, oh so tired. "She's still not awake."

"No, she's not. But we are going to take her off the vent today. She's breathing on her own. That's a big improvement. Her bruises are healed, the scars minimal from all the stitches she received."

"And the burns?"

"They're healing nicely. They weren't as bad as they could have been, that's for sure." The doctor takes a deep breath, exhales. "Mr. Kramer, this is all good news. Like I told you on day one, one step at a time, okay?"

"Yeah, right."

*Don't you dare die on me.*

*Don't you dare di—*

A tugging sensation fills my throat until it triggers my gag reflex. My body convulses as I cough, my throat burning like it did when I was inhaling smoke.

"Doc, she's coughing." Squirrel is still here. "Is that normal?"

My lid is lifted and bright light flashes in one eye, then the other. I can see light! It's not a dark hole in here anymore.

Wait, am I waking up from a coma? Is that what this is?

I tell myself to open my eyes, one at a time. They're so heavy. It feels impossible a task, but I can't give up. Squirrel didn't give up, begged me to live. Well, guess what? I lived. Now I just need to wake up.

*Don't you dare die on me.*

I try again to open my eyes, and this time they flutter. Shadows dance briefly in front of me. I try again and again until they stay open.

"Well hello there."

A man leans over me, one I don't recognize. But his voice is familiar.

"I'm Dr. Smith. Welcome back."

I open my mouth to speak, but nothing comes out but a dry croak. A glass of water is thrust in front of me from my other side, and I roll my neck to see who's holding it.

"Squi—"

"Miss Cantor, let's try to drink the water. See if that helps."

## Squirrel

Squirrel holds the straw to my lips, and I greedily drink the cool liquid, my eyes never leaving him.

"Better?" Squirrel asks.

I nod.

"I'll give you two a minute. The nurse will be in to check on you soon."

The doctor's footsteps retreat until the door closes. Still, I don't look away from Squirrel.

"You scared the shit out of me, Lexi."

Squirrel's words are accusatory, but his tone tells a different story.

"I'm sorry," I say hoarsely.

His eyes narrow, a crease forming on his brow. He looks like he's aged ten years since I last saw him.

Since I last saw him...

"How long?"

"What?"

"How long have I been out?" I ask.

Squirrel lowers his head. "It doesn't matter." When he lifts his eyes to lock onto mine, it's impossible to miss the sheen.

"Squirrel, how long?"

"Three and a half weeks."

I swallow past the lump in my throat. It's a lot easier than dealing with a tube, that's for sure.

"You were here the entire time."

Squirrel's eyes widen. "How'd you know?"

I smile. "I heard you. I heard a lot of people, but mostly you."

"The doctor's said you might be able to hear me. I kept talking, just in case."

"I'm glad you did. But even when I couldn't hear you

here, I heard you. Over and over again I heard you saying 'Don't you dare die on me'. That kept me going."

Squirrel lifts my hand gently, presses a kiss to my palm.

"I need to tell you something," he says.

"I know. Alan is dead. You're sorry. I heard it all, Squirrel. There's nothing left to tell me."

"Well, yeah, all that, but..." He shakes his head. "That's not what I was going to say."

"Oh."

"You need to know that I love you, Lexi. I'm not going to lie and say I knew right away. But when I saw you on the ground? When Alan was doing his best to kill you? An image of me as an old man flashed in my head and it about broke me when you weren't standing next to me. I realized then that I don't want a life without you. Because I love you. So fucking much."

My heart pounds, but this time it's for all the right reasons.

"I love you too, Squirrel." I grin. "Which is good considering you already moved me into your house."

Squirrel throws his head back, laughing so hard. I soak up the sound, making sure that it's what I hear playing on a loop in my brain from here on out. No more words of death. No more begging for life.

Only Squirrel. Always Squirrel.

# Epilogue

*I promise.*

**Squirrel**

*Four weeks later...*

"You're not even dressed yet."

I turn from the closet to see Lexi standing in the doorway, a towel wrapped around her. I cross my arms over my chest and grin.

"Neither are you."

"I just got out of the shower. Of course I'm not dressed yet." She tilts her head. "What's your excuse?"

"One more quickie before we go?"

"How many quickies do you need in one day? There was the one this morning, then again after lunch. And let's not forget the one fifteen minutes ago... in the damn shower."

"I will never get enough."

"You can't survive on sex alone, Squirrel. And neither can I." She crosses the room and wraps her arms around my waist, pressing her cheek to my chest. "I know you're making up for lost time, but—"

"Eight weeks, Lexi," I remind her. "I'm making up for eight weeks. You were just cleared a few days ago. We still have a long way to go."

"And we will, but not tonight," she says, pushing away from me. "Tonight, we celebrate."

"Are you sure you're up for a party?" I ask, concern etching my tone. "Maybe we should put it off for another week or so. I don't want you to overdo it."

"If I overdo it, Squirrel, it'll be because of all the sex we had, not a few drinks at the clubhouse with everyone." She smiles. "Please, I need this. I've been cooped up in this house for weeks. I want to see everyone, celebrate my officially becoming the club's attorney. Don't ruin this for me."

Fender offered her the job a week ago. He presented her with another contract, one that detailed much more of what she'd be dealing with if she agreed to be on retainer for the club. Of course she negotiated the terms. She even got him to agree to monthly meetings with voting members of the club so she could be kept in the loop about anything that might come up legally.

I know that there will be a lot that she's never privy to, and if she's being honest, so does she. She just doesn't seem to care.

She also convinced him that the club should open up a legal clinic in town. One that would allow her to represent others who might not be able to afford representation otherwise. We've all seen how corrupt the system can be, and this is her way of doing something about it. Even if it is just a small piece in the larger puzzle.

"I'm not going to ruin anything for you. I just worry, that's all."

## Squirrel

"I know you do. And I love you for it. But really, I'm fine." She walks out the door, calling over her shoulder, "Now get dressed."

I let out a groan but return to the closet to find something to wear. After a few minutes, Bug comes running in the room and plops at my feet, letting out a whine.

"I know, Bug. I'm not gonna find shit in here, am I?"

I move from the closet to the dresser. I settle on jeans and a red Henley. I grab my cut off the end of the bed and put it on.

Bug lifts his head and barks.

"Perfect, right?"

I head out to the living room where my boots are and put them on. A quick glance at the clock tells me I've managed to kill all of five minutes. I resign myself to waiting on Lexi to finish getting ready.

Another hour passes before I hear the bathroom door open. I jump up from the couch and turn toward the hall. My mouth goes dry, and my tongue sticks to the roof of it.

*Holy fuck!*

My gaze travels the length of her, taking in the familiar outfit.

On Lexi's feet are the same three-inch red spiked heels she had on all those months ago back in Michigan in that little shop downtown. The dark wash jeans with rips up the length of them and the tight red tee that has the deepest V at the neck I've ever seen fit her body like a glove.

"You look..." I shake my head, unable to find the right word.

"Sexy, amazing, stunning... any one of those work," she teases.

"All of those."

"Thank you." Her smile is wide, bright and beautiful.

"There's only one thing missing."

Lexi's smile falls. "How?" she cries. "I'm wearing everything I was that day. There's nothing more I had—"

I lift her glasses from the end table where she left them earlier and hold them out to her. "These."

"Oh, right."

She takes them and settles them on her nose.

"Better?" she asks.

"Perfect."

I close the distance between us and lift her into my arms. I carry her to the nearest wall and pin her there.

"What are you doing?"

"One last quickie, Lexi. I promise."

# Next in the Soulless Kings MC Series

### Gibson: Book 8

**Gibson...**

As a former military medic and the doc for the Soulless Kings MC, I've seen a lot. More than most ER doctors for sure. And treating the Bangin' Betties comes with the territory. They don't exactly live clean lives, but it's not my place to judge. And what they do outside of the clubhouse isn't my business... until it is.

When one of the Bangin' Betties shows up on my doorstep in the middle of the night, beaten and barely clinging to life, I fall back on my training. I don't think, I just act. In doing so, I open up a world of chaos I wasn't prepared for. I don't know what's worse: the mayhem that ensues or the fact that my heart doesn't seem to care that I'm falling in love with the woman who caused it.

**Alena...**

Whore. Prostitute. Slut. It doesn't matter what people call me as long as I get paid at the end of the night. Unless

## Next in the Soulless Kings MC Series

I'm at the Soulless Kings clubhouse. There I'm a Bangin' Betty and I don't charge. Because they may be wild, but they treat the Betties with respect. I'm not a commodity to them, and realizing I'm worth more than fifty bucks for a back-alley blowjob, I decide to make a change.

Unfortunately, I'm my pimp's highest earner, which isn't saying much. When he tries to *convince* me to stay, I know I only have one option: Soulless Kings MC. By some miracle, I made it to the club's property and their doc's house. But now that he's fixed me up, I realize I have an entirely different problem.

Did I just leave one pimp behind only to be used by the very people I thought I could trust? Or, for the first time in my life, should I trust my gut and give the doc and the Kings a chance?

# About the Author

Andi Rhodes is an author whose passion is creating romance from chaos in all her books! She writes MC (motorcycle club) romance with a generous helping of suspense and doesn't shy away from the more difficult topics. Her books can be triggering for some so consider yourself warned. Andi also ensures each book ends with the couple getting their HEA! Most importantly, Andi is living her real life HEA with her husband and their boxers.

For access to release info, updates, and exclusive content, be sure to sign up for Andi's newsletter at andirhodes.com.

# Also by Andi Rhodes

**Broken Rebel Brotherhood**

Broken Souls

Broken Innocence

Broken Boundaries

Broken Rebel Brotherhood: Complete Series Box set

**Broken Rebel Brotherhood: Next Generation**

Broken Hearts

Broken Wings

Broken Mind

**Bastards and Badges**

Stark Revenge

Slade's Fall

Jett's Guard

**Soulless Kings MC**

Fender

Joker

Piston

Greaser

Riker

Trainwreck

Squirrel

Gibson

## Satan's Legacy MC

Snow's Angel

Toga's Demons

Magic's Torment

Printed in Great Britain
by Amazon